2⁵⁰

PENGUIN BOOKS
ROOM SERVICE

Frank Moorhouse was born in Nowra, New
South Wales. In the last few years he has moved
around both Australia and the world, reading his
stories at festivals, working as a writer-in-
residence and as a reporter. He visited the
Middle East peace-keeping force in the Sinai
Desert, went into Lebanon during the siege of
Beirut, and has been a cultural exchange writer
to India and China. He covered the New
Orleans and other mardi gras for the *Bulletin,*
and was for a time its nightclub writer. He goes
for long stretches into the bush, backpacking.

His writing has won numerous prizes including
the National Award for Fiction, and the Henry
Lawson Short Story Prize. He was made a
member of the Order of Australia in 1985 for his
services to literature.

D1113551

Futility and Other Animals
The Americans, Baby
The Electrical Experience
Conference-ville
Tales of Mystery and Romance
The Everlasting Secret Family and Other Secrets
Days of Wine and Rage

FRANK MOORHOUSE

ROOM SERVICE

PENGUIN BOOKS

Penguin Books Australia Ltd,
487 Maroondah Highway, P.O. Box 257
Ringwood, Victoria, 3134, Australia
Penguin Books Ltd,
Harmondsworth, Middlesex, England
Penguin Books,
40 West 23rd Street, New York, N.Y. 10010. U.S.A.
Penguin Books Canada Ltd,
2801 John Street, Markham, Ontario, Canada L3R 1B4
Penguin Books (N.Z.) Ltd,
182-190 Wairau Road, Auckland 10, New Zealand

First published 1985 by Viking
Published in Penguin, 1987

Typeset in 11/13 Bembo Roman by Leader Composition Pty. Ltd.
Offset from the Viking edition
Made and printed in Australia by
Australian Print Group, Maryborough, Victoria

CIP

Moorhouse, Frank, 1938–
Room service.

ISBN 0 14 010198 5.

I. Title.

A823'.3

To Susie Carleton
friend, patron of the arts

Contents

··

PART 2: ORAL HISTORY OF A CHILDHOOD

PART 3: DEATH: REMEDIES: CONVALESCENCE

PART ONE

TALES FROM
SWIZZLESTICK

THE NEW YORK BELL CAPTAIN
···

In New York City, at the old Times Square Hotel, I place my six bottles of Heineken beer along the window sill to chill in snow, to save the 50-cent ice charge, to avoid filling the hand-basin with ice and beer, and to spare myself the sight of the bell captain's outstretched palm. I then leave my room to push my way along the Manhattan streets through the muggers, but change my mind at the hotel door and the snow and return, instead, to drink my Heineken. Reaching the room I find the beer gone from the sill. Instantly, without a flicker of hesitation, I know that the bell captain has swiftly checked my room to find out if I am using the window sill to chill my beer instead of paying him 50 cents plus tip to bring up a plastic bag full of melting ice. Quick work on his part. I open out the window to look for clues and as I do the six bottles of Heineken are swept off the sill down fifteen stories into Fifty-Fourth Street – and the bad end of Fifty-Fourth. I am too apathetic to bother looking down. Already New York is dehumanising me. And I've lost my beer. At first I think it is all my mistake – that when

I first looked for the beer I looked at the wrong window. That I then opened the right window in the wrong way and pushed them off. (May be a lot of the so-called muggings in New York are really head injuries from falling bottles from hotel windows sills because hungry-handed bell captains charge too much for ice). But as I sit there bereft and brooding I arrive at a more convincing conclusion about the beer, the sill, the window. What the bell captain has done is to come into my room, find the bottles, steal one or two or even three and then switch them to where I will sweep the remaining bottles off. This way I will never know if he has been into my room to steal my beer. I will therefore be unable to bring substantiated allegations against him. Alright. This round to the bell captain.

DEPOSITION TWO

I have proved that the bell captain provides ice which is at melting point. I suspected this from the start. The first time I ordered ice I paid him 50 cents, tipped him, checked my wallet, latched and locked the door and propped a chair against it, when I turned around all I had was a plastic bag of ice-water. So I did this. I bought a bag of ice from the drugstore next door to the hotel and sat there in my room and timed its melting against another bag of the bell captain's ice. The results were inconclusive but down in the bell captain's den, I am convinced that they leave the ice out of the freezer to bring it just to melting point and they give this ice to non-tippers or a person who doesn't tip 'enough' for bell captains. I have a frustrated urge to hand them my wallet, to put my wallet in the hand of the bell captain and ask him to take what he thinks is 'fair'. I was told of a man who had no hands and who kept his money in that unused outside breast pocket of his suit (which schoolboys, railway clerks, electricity-meter readers, and eccentrics use sensibly for pens and pencils) so that taxi drivers and so on could help themselves to the money. Poor bastard. Perhaps I should pull my hands into my sleeves and let New York help itself.

DEPOSITION THREE

Anyhow, what can they do to you if you don't tip? What they do in New York is they turn off the heat to your room. Can they do that? Is that mechanically possible – can they isolate one room out of six hundred and turn off its heat? Well they did it to my room. They must have a control panel down in the bell captain's den.

DEPOSITION FOUR

Every afternoon I have a conversation through the keyhole with the maid who wants me to leave the room so that she can 'change the linen'. When am I going out, she inquires. For 'change the linen' read: Allow the bell captain to come in and prowl about my room and steal my Heineken beer. We come to an arrangement. I take my Heineken in my brief case and sit in the lobby while she 'changes the linen'.

DEPOSITION FIVE

Oh, they know that Francois Blase is just a *nom de voyage*. I know I have not fooled them. The word has gone around too that we are exchange-rate millionaires. Bell captains study the exchange rate. In a ploy to extract larger tips the bell captain has told the doorman to stop opening the door for me, despite a tip of 75 cents the previous evening for bringing up half a dozen Heineken and a packet of crackerjack. When I didn't order ice they knew I was using the window sill.

When I suspect the doorman is not opening the door for me as a reprimand for using the window sill and not buying melted ice from them, I sit in the lobby and count the comings and goings and the times the doorman opens the door. To confirm my suspicions. He opens the door every time. I then rise from my chair in the lobby and go to the door, even saying something genial about the Miami Dolphins and the League to show my immersion in the life of the United States and to show that I bear no ideological or other objections and so on. The bell captain pretends not to hear and the doorman pretends to answer the telephone. I have to open the door myself. The first of twelve comings and goings that the doorman had not opened the door. I 'turn on my heel' and return to my room, deeply miffed.

DEPOSITION SIX

I eat, imprudently, in the lobby restaurant as I do not feel like going out that much – things to do in my room and so on. Obviously the waiter ignores me on the whisper from the bell captain, despite my dollar tip to him for sending a cable home for more money so that I could continue to tip the hotel staff. I eventually have to lean from my chair and grab the waiter's sleeve and jacket with both my hands pulling him to an unsteady halt and me nearly out of my chair. With many smiles, bowing and scrapings, I say that I am going to the theatre and am therefore in a rush. He says what, at 5.45? But anyhow I get some service. Except that what I ask for is off, he says, although I think I see others being served it, and I think he brings me something other than what I ordered, but it takes so

long I can't really remember what I ordered. At least I get my
Heineken. Of course, I am being penalised for some breach of
the hotel customs. I leave a 27-per-cent tip as a gesture of my
willingness to 'get along'.

DEPOSITION SEVEN

I eat in the lobby restaurant again, not feeling like going out
because I see a blizzard hiding behind the clouds waiting to lash
out at me. This time the restaurant pulls a switch in behaviour
to throw me into anguish and confusion. On a signal from the
bell captain which I did not see, the waiter serves me, this time,
too quickly. A masquerade – uncivilised haste masquerading as
promptness. They want to get me out of the restaurant, get me
to rush my food. They don't like me because I dawdle over my
food with a book. Hah! They don't like people who read books
at dinner. They think, maybe, I am 'parading' my bookishness.
So, it's the book-reading that sticks in their gut.

Despite the rushed service, I tip heavily again. I do this for
three reasons: to preserve the good name of dinner-table book-
readers; to show that I am above pettiness; and to make them
think that maybe we are the world's fastest eaters as well as
being best at everything else. In short to repay confusion with
confusion.

I stand in the lobby picking my teeth, here it is only 6.15 and
I've eaten a three-course dinner. I toy with the idea of going out
and sparring with the people of New York, turning the table on
a few muggers, but decide to go back to my room and have a
quiet Heinie and watch colour TV. The bell captain and
doorman smile, tip their caps, bow and so on – all unfelt
gestures, a debasement of the body-language of service. I know
they don't care. The doorman even goes through the motions
of opening the lift door, which is automatic. I tip him without

looking to see if he smiles or says thankyou, and without consulting my Chamber of Commerce Guide to tipping in automatic lifts.

DEPOSITION EIGHT

A stranger in the lobby asks me for change for the 'valet' slot machine. I at first pretend not to hear, a New York reflex, knowing that as soon as I reach for my money I will betray the amount that I carry, as soon as I speak he will know where I come from and am therefore rich and generous and foolish, and that Francois Blase is a cover, and that whatever I do will reveal me as naive and paranoiac. There is something else, I fear, which I call New York Sleight of Hand, which will make whatever I have disappear. He persists in what appears to be a civilised, middle-class way, so I give him a handful of change. He offers me a note. I wave it away. He thanks me wonderously and goes to the valet machine, looking back at me and back to his handful of money. At first I feel pleased with myself – it is this sort of gesture that gets us a good name. But when I glance over to the bell captain he appears to be scowling and refuses to meet my eyes. I enter the lift, troubled. In the lift it dawns on me. It is his job to give change and, anyhow, the valet machine is an automation of hotel employment and is probably declared black by the hotel staff. How stupid of me. I have robbed the bell captain of a quarter tip; diminished his role; and threatened his employment. I feel chilly. For these things I will have to pay.

DEPOSITION NINE

When I get to my room the heat is off. Apart from the obvious offences like giving change in the lobby, using the window sill to chill beer, I must have done other offensive things. I rove over my dealings with the hotel staff and my mind recalls to me the automatic lift. One lift is automatic and the other is run by a one-armed black. I have preference for the automatic lift and this must count against me. Maybe I should use the one-armed black lift driver to keep him in employment, as an endorsement of the human element in mechanised society, and as a gesture against discrimination. Maybe I should tip the black lift driver too, although my information from the Chamber of Commerce is that lift drivers are not tipped. Next time, I go by the one-armed black's lift and I see that he is selling the Sunday *New York Times* and I buy a copy from him, although I worry about the newpaper seller in the lobby who is blind and what he will think. The one-armed lift driver charges me 75 cents for the 50-cent paper. With some sort of neurotic reversed-response (like those who smile involuntarily when informed of tragedy), I apologise and thank the one-armed black lift driver. What about the blind paper seller?

DEPOSITION TEN

I am, I tell myself, too passive before the minor oppressions. I am always virtuously assertive about the major oppressions of our times. Apartheid, you name it. But I remain timid before the accumulated indignities which sour the quality of life. I adopt a pretentious inner attitude of 'Pooh, I have not the mental time to worry about the miscellaneous petty injustices of the day-to-day world. My life is dedicated to a larger mission'. So I let waiters off.

I resolve to change this. I go down and confront the manager when my heat is off on the third afternoon. I begin by saying that I know all about Traveller Paranoia and that I have tested myself. I am not suffering from Traveller Paranoia. I want, I tell him, no accusations of that sort.

The depositions of my journal, which I produce as Exhibit A, and the whole heat business, clearly make a case against the bell captain and I call for his dismissal.

I refer the manager to the case of *Jackson* v. *Horizon Holidays Ltd*. A person who books a holiday at a hotel which falls short of the brochure description can claim damages for vexation and disappointment.

People throughout the world, I thunder, have for too long taken advantage of our open, relaxed, simplified, small-country responses to life. For too long now we have been known as 'easy going'. Because we inhabit a rich, technologically advanced, uncrowded, clean country we are resented and penalised.

I close my case.

'About the economics and geography of your country I know nothing, Mr Blase, but as for the heat – this is a fuel saving measure introduced because of the world fuel situation. Between eleven and three, we turn off the heat. It is the warmest part of the day. Also, most people are usually out of their rooms at around these times.'

I stare at him.

I marvel at the ingenuity of his defence.

Alright, I say, this time I'll accept what you say and, 'turning on my heel', I go back to my room.

I need time to pick apart this carefully prepared explanation.

SUMMING UP

Later, brooding in my cold room, the point of his last remark comes to me, 'most people are usually out of their rooms at around these times'.

What business is it of anyone that I have not left the hotel precincts for five days or so? Do I go out and be mugged on the streets of Manhattan so that the bell captain can have a free hand with the thieving of my Heineken? So they can pick over my luggage. I rent the room. I don't have to go out to see landmarks every day of my life. Anyhow, everything that happens on a journey is 'experience'. It doesn't have to be all landmarks and monuments. Maybe, for all they know, I am exploring the inner spaces of my mind, the subterranean caves of my personality, gazing with new understanding at the ruins and monuments of my own archaeology. The seven wonders of the heart. What would the staff of the old Times Square Hotel know about that? Nothing. Nothing at all.

THE INDIAN BELL CAPTAIN
....

Probably through an American aid program, most of the Western hotels in India now have bell captains. As a world traveller and cultural delegate, this dismayed me. I have warred with bell captains in many US cities and believe it is the traveller's job to re-train bell captains. On my last trip I experimented to see how much it would take in tips to make an American bell captain grin but had to leave the experiment unconcluded.

India, however, is a different question.

My first understanding of the Indian bell captain question came in Hyderabad. I wanted to post two cards to Australia and tried to buy stamps at Reception, but they directed me to the 'bell captain'.

Bell captains in India smile at you, unlike US bell captains who, having an optical defect, cannot see you. As George Kaufman said on the death of the head bell captain at the Algonquin in New York, 'I don't know how God did it'.

'What do you mean?' asked Dorothy Parker.

'How did God catch his eye?'

Catching the eye of the bell captain in the US requires gymnastics. I found that I have to manoeuvre myself into the field of vision of the bell captain without getting behind his desk and without taking his head in my hands. Sometimes I found myself leaning over the bell captain's desk, an elbow nonchalantly on the counter, chin in hand, leaning so far as to have one foot off the ground.

Perhaps to lie on the bell captain's desk might have been another way.

But the Indian bell captain, I found, was a different problem entirely. It was how to keep the bell captain's eyes off me.

If I tried to do anything, tie a shoe lace, the bell captain would be there.

And unlike the US bell captain, he did not put his hand into your pocket, take out the wallet, remove the tip, and put it back.

If the Indian bell captain thinks he is not going to get a tip, he looks hungry, dispirited. On the way out of the room without a tip he is likely to stumble with fatigue, lean weakly in the doorway, cough pitiably, spit blood into a handkerchief. He might even fall and have to be helped up, saying, 'it is nothing, I will rest for one moment'.

Foreign Affairs advise me to tip about 2 rupees for service (about 20 cents), but other Australians told me that this could be got down by haggling. Australians, of course, resent tipping because they never know how much to tip.

I found that if I over-tipped bell captains in the US I got service but it was service with contempt because the bell captain knew that he had me beaten.

If you over-tip an Indian bell captain he will move into your room.

He will send in the sweepers, the valet, they will spray for mosquitoes, polish the drinking glasses, take the telephone to pieces and clean it, replace the sheets while you're still in the bed, gesturing with a hand, 'No – to leave the bed is not necessary, please remain', and as two assistants gently lift you the bed will be made under you.

But it was the problem of the postage stamps which caused my only doubts and suspicions about the bell captains.

There were stories from other travellers about the postage stamp racket. And letters in the Indian newspapers said that anyone who handled mail was likely to remove the uncancelled stamps and throw the mail away (and this presumably included bell captains). As one letter in the *Hindu* said, 'The outgoing foreign mail was not infrequently tampered with for collection of the stamps affixed thereto resulting in the mails never reaching their intended destination. And, nothing used to be heard of them or their fate.'

To forestall this temptation in the Indian bell captain, I intended to buy the stamps and post them personally.

The bell captain was young, perhaps still in training.

'Where to sir?'

'Australia.'

'Ah – back in Australia you are a cricketer perhaps?'

'No.'

'Would I be asking a personal question if I enquired of you why it is that you do not play cricket?'

'I was no good at it.'

'Surely not sir, you have the build of a cricketer, a very fine cricketer perhaps.'

'Thankyou – stamps – do you have stamps?'

'Sir – which is the finest cricket team in the whole world?'

That was easy, 'India – definitely India,' I replied.

'No sir, you say that to flatter me, to flatter India. The answer sir, is the West Indies.'

'Thankyou. How much is it airmail to Australia?'

'Unfortunately I have no 1-rupee stamps but we will solve it.'

He went to his stamp folder and produced eighteen 20-paise

stamps, 'We will make do, never mind. We will get the mails through.'

'But they will not fit on the card – nine stamps will not fit,' I said, 'there is no room.'

'Not to worry – they will fit – you see. If it is fine by you sir, I will not lick these stamps, for reason of hygiene.'

'It is alright, I will put on the stamps.'

But I knew they wouldn't fit.

'No sir, it is my duty to place the stamps.'

Hah, I thought, I will not move until the stamps *have* been placed.

I would stay anyhow just to see how they could possibly be fitted onto the postcard. The Lord's Prayer can be written on the back of a postage stamp, my knowledge of Hindi can be written on the back of a postage stamp, but I could not see how this postcard of Hyderabad's Rotary Park could fit onto the backs of nine 20-paise stamps without losing either the address or the message.

The bell captain separated the eighteen stamps individually and laid them out on the glass top of his desk.

He took from a locked cupboard, a jar of clag with a huge brush.

He began to paint the backs of the stamps liberally with glue; the glue overlapped the stamps onto the glass top.

He smiled at me, 'This will prevent theft of the stamps from the postcards between here and the destination.'

The bell captain then had trouble getting the individual stamps off the glass top of the counter because the glue was making them very wet. He smiled again, 'Small problem.'

He slid them along the glass counter and off the edge where they stuck. He then used a finger nail to lift them off. He smiled at me, 'Please, easily done.'

The stamps had picked up a little grime in their journey across the glass top, but you could still see that they were stamps.

The bell captain then had trouble getting the stamps off his gluey fingers. While he held the card he also gave the stamps a second coat of glue. And so with the other eight stamps. As I had calculated the stamps did not fit. I looked away to ease the bell captain's embarrassment. When I looked back the stamps were all in place, pasted over the address.

'The stamps are in place but you will see that we have lost the address,' the bell captain said, still smiling, 'but I will rectify that.'

He went on with the second card, slopping the stamps generously with glue and fixing them on the card. The first card had been placed down on the glass top in the swamp of glue and the ink was running. Both cards looked as if they had been left out in the rain. The bell captain finished the second card and found that the first card had adhered to the glass counter.

The glue, however, was still fluid enough to allow it to be slid off the counter. The bell captain wiped off the excess glue with his sleeve, blurring the message and wiping off two of the stamps, which stuck to his sleeve. 'Oh dear,' he said, looking at me with a resigned smile.

He peeled them off his sleeve and fixed them back on the card after giving them a good slopping with glue.

At this point a clerk came to the bell captain with the autographs of the Australian cricket team. The bell captain became interested in the autographs and placed both the cards down in the swamp of glue on the glass top of his desk.

I rescued the two cards before they became permanently stuck to the glass top. I took them to another table and tried to reprint the addresses, but found the cards too soggy to take ink. I leaned back, wiped away the perspiration from my brow and muttered a mantra.

The bell captain came running over, 'Sir, I will do the mailing of the cards.'

I said no, it was alright, and I took the cards to the lift with the bell captain following, hurt, 'Sir, it is my duty.'

'But I have to let the cards dry so that I can reprint the addresses.'

'No sir, I will do that for you. That was my plan. You tell me the address and I will print it.'

He took out a ball-point pen.

'No, it is OK,' I said, tipping him, 'please – thankyou.'

'I will not accept the tip, sir, until I have competed the task.'

I reached my room, gently eased the bell captain and the others out of my room and closed the door. I could hear them outside, discussing the matter among themselves with mutual recrimination.

I placed the two sodden cards on the air-conditioning outlet and they dried within the hour, although they curled. They were heavier, too, from the coating of glue and probably required additional postage. I printed the address in minute script around the stamps on the remaining space. I had no confidence in their arrival.

Later in the bar (for a holy person the bar is a holy place) I asked an Indian friend, 'Why did the bell captain use the glue? Was it for hygiene, because he didn't want to lick the stamps, or was it to make it harder for someone to steal the stamps? Did it make them removable so that if I had left them with him he could have peeled them off? Which was it?'

My Indian friend said that none of these was the answer – the bell captain used glue because the stamps had been stolen from other mail and consequently had no glue.

'Why did he handle the glue so badly?' I asked.

My Indian friend quoted from the novel *The Serpent and the Rope* by Indian writer Raja Rao. In the novel the Indian character allows his French wife to pack the luggage into the car and to drive the car, saying, 'How incompetent we Indians felt before *things*.'

HILTONIA
··············

As you know, Chief, I do not knock people who stay at the Hilton chain while travelling (or 'Tip Town' as it is known among its devotees). I myself have a fondness for chain motels and am something of a specialist in Ramada Inns, Travelodge, Howard Johnsons, and Holiday Inns. I know the inadequacies of the less than intrepid traveller. I know about Traveller Paranoia, imaginary bed bugs, asbestos moneybelts. And you may remember too that last vacation I stayed at my hometown Hilton in Sydney. But there is something else I want to say about the Hiltons – they are themselves a travelling experience. They are another country. The Sydney Hilton is not Sydney. Rarely do you hear or see an Australian at the Sydney Hilton, the voices you hear are Japanese or American and the staff are foreign. The Hilton concept also contributes to an ethnic shuffling with its menus and decor – it severs you from nationality. So the restaurant in Sydney is the San Francisco, the Istanbul Hilton has an English pub inside it, and in France the Hilton at Orly has a restaurant called La Louisiane in a Mississippi river-boat setting.

I like the bidets in the foreign Hiltons with their erotic

possibilities, I like room service Suzy Wong sandwiches (available, as far as I know, only at the Istanbul Hilton) and, of course, the universal club sandvic (as we say in Istanbul). Give me a club sandvic, a complimentary Hilton bubble bath, a dozen Heineken, and maybe a butterscotch sundae and I can find inner peace – going now and then, of course, to the balcony.

My holiday last year was at the Sydney Hilton. I'm such a bad holidayer. I play no sport, have trouble making friends in the lifts of strange hotels in strange countries. I don't get along with bell captains. I have trouble lying in the sun – I think I can do it, but I get over-hot. I lie there thinking too much, I think of things 'to do' and things I've done wrong.

At the Hilton I could invite friends up for drinks from the automated bar in my room. I knew the best restaurants. I had the Sydney library over the road run by my friends Sara Walters and Fay Lawrence. I had the hotel pool. Massage service. The John Valentine Health Club was closed so thankfully I couldn't do my jogging.

My window looked out on my house in Balmain so I could watch for robbers and see who cared enough to call on me.

You don't hear an Australian voice in the Hilton, so you can pull the curtains and forget you're in Australia.

I sat in front of the television watching midday movies and re-runs of *Upstairs Downstairs* and *The Streets of San Francisco* and drank and ate my way through the room-service menu, beginning with the first entree and the first main course and working my way meal by meal through the menu during the week. I even got to play cards with the room-service staff.

But before I do the report on the Hiltonia I think I owe it to everyone to explain Blase's Theory of Pure Travel.

Travelling is essentially the act of travelling – not the destination or the monuments.

As Brecht says, 'It is the journey not the destination'. Travelling is really about bookings, tickets, finding out how the taps work, power points, tipping, driving the autobahn, street maps, and timetables and meeting other lonely travellers in bars, such as Mr Casapolla, from Sicily, who is an expert on liquid-waste disposal.

But I don't think it's about getting the best rate of exchange, avoiding being overcharged at restaurants or worrying about the taxi drivers taking you the long way around. That's all a very wasteful sort of worry.

But for me, Chief, the essential part of travelling is meeting the inconsequential, face to face. I know Donald Horne has published a book about the museums of Europe. I want to write a sequel called *Inconsequential Europe*. I seem to spend so much of my time with the inconsequential and I find that looking at monuments worries me. I try too hard with monuments. I read too much before and after, or I worry that I haven't read enough or that I've clouded my mind with historical background and can't 'see' the monument for itself.

I worry that I've missed some curious detail. I know from having seen 5000 cathedrals, 2000 Indian temples, and so many crusader forts, that there are curious details which everyone misses except those who know all about curious details which are 'the whole point of it'. Someone tells you about what you've missed around the pool later on.

But back to Hiltonia. My most political Hiltonian experience so far was in the Tel Aviv Hilton where I was involved in a political demonstration by the Hilton residents.

My last Hilton demonstration was in Athens where I was trapped by an anti-American demonstration which surrounded the hotel (like an 'angry sea', I think my story said). I watched it from the twelfth floor with my ouzo. No, I lie. The last was when I was caught up in a demonstration against John Kerr, a former Governor-General, at the Sydney Hilton where I happened to be an afternoon guest with a dear friend.

But in Tel Aviv the demonstration was inside the King Solomon Grill. I was in the Grill when I heard a New York Jewish woman say that some people she knew had cancelled their vacation in Israel this year because of the trouble in Lebanon.

'We didn't cancel this year because of the trouble,' she said. 'We felt we should come, trouble or without trouble. We owe it that we should share this with them.'

I realised then that simply staying at the Tel Aviv Hilton was a political act. This was confirmed later in the bar by a Californian architect named Rene who wasn't staying at the Hilton. He was staying up the road at the Sheraton. ' I do my playing at a hotel other than my own,' he said. He explained that he didn't like the barman and the doorman or whoever knowing what he was up to: 'If you pick up a chick from your own hotel and it doesn't work out you have to face her in the lift or at the pool next day.' Anyhow, Rene said that it was a common attitude among American Jews that to come to Israel this year was an act of political support for Israel's foreign policy. So while I was having my fifth martini in the King Solomon Grill (where I hung out) I was in a political demonstration. It was the nicest demonstration I've been in.

I did the one-day American Express tour to Sodom which was full of Australian hairdressers. I was told I'd have to organise the trip to Onan myself.

I then checked out the Cairo Rameses Hilton. When people from another country meet you as a visitor they assume that, as an intelligent traveller, what you want to 'do' is a cathedral, followed by a castle, and then a crusader fort. That's all very well and educational, I suppose, but what Francois Blase wants to do, if the truth be known, say here in Cairo, is to shimmy at the disco where King Farouk used to shimmy. He was a bon vivant of the 1950s. He was our hero at Wollongong Tech. I'd like to ring some of the numbers he used to ring but I suppose those numbers would have changed and they'd be all married by now.

Here in Cairo at the Rameses Hilton I hang out at the Club 36 with Gergius and Tadros, the barmen. They are forever telling me to see monuments.

They insist I see the pyramids. But I say to them that to watch them construct a cocktail tells me more about Egyptian culture than the pyramids. Tadros makes the Seth and it's incredible. Seth was God of the Desert. A Seth is gin, sweet vermouth, orange, cherry brandy and bitter lemon. It's garnished with a whole lime, unpeeled like a mummy, so that the peel winds its way through the drink, like a veil dancer. Pinned to the lime, which is wedged into the huge glass, are a cherry and a lemon slice and two red-plastic monkeys, one hanging from the other by its tail.

You drink it through two long thin straws – one pink, one green. It's a dazzling construction.

'Tadros,' I said, 'where did you learn to do this marvellous thing?'

'You admire?'

'Very much. I like the way it embodies the colors of the Nile sunset, the flamboyant variety of the market place, the eroticism of the Arabian veil dancer, and it carries the suggestion of mystic potions from ancient times – elixirs and poisons. It is *jameel* [beautiful]. Where did you learn this?'

'From the Hilton Cocktail School,' he said, proudly.

Next to me a couple of girls on holiday from a kibbutz in Israel talk with a couple of Englishmen who are driving across Africa. One of the girls says she's 'fitting in as much as she can.'

One of the guys says, 'You have to get as much done as you can while you're here.'

They agree that it's a pity to waste time when there's so much to see.

I worry that in all the places I've been in my life I have never 'seen everything' I should have seen.

All I've done in Cairo, apart from shimmying at the nightclub King Farouk used to shimmy at, is to install my travellers' survival kit, put together by Viking Industries of Yonkers NY ($34.95). It has a dual ionization smoke detector and an anti-intrusion alarm, which you wedge under the door, and a how-to-survive-a-hotel-fire manual. But they don't tell you about air raids. In the Tel Aviv Hilton they have air-raid shelters. I did my air-raid drill, but I seemed to be the only one.

I found myself with a fantasy in the Istanbul Hilton. An announcement would come over Turkish radio saying that there was unrest in the streets and all foreigners were to stay in their hotels indefinitely. That would be fine for me – to watch civil unrest from the balcony of a Hilton with a Heineken.

In the Istanbul foyer there are probably more currency deals going than in the London Hilton. I was offered some good illegal deals in the foyer of the Istanbul Hilton (double the bank-rate), but I mentioned the words 'firing squad' in Turkish. The currency dealer merely shrugged in a 'characteristically Turkish way' and said that that was the risk you took for double the bank-rate. But what I wanted to tell you about was the day I took the Istanbul Hilton lobby Tour B. Maybe it was just a ragged day for Tour B and I don't offer this as a general critique because I do not often take lobby tours. This was Tour B (no lecture) up the Bosporus and did not include a Light and Sound show either. The Hilton lobby in Athens offers an Acropolis by Moonlight tour '. . . on the two days preceding the full moon, full night and one day after the full moon when there is no Sound and Light show, the tour will include instead a visit to the Acropolis by moonlight . . .' But I wander. I took Tour B (no lecture) up the Bosporus, as the old joke goes, it is easy to forget where you are in the Hilton. This tour began with an air-conditioned motor coach from the hotel, to the motor launch in the Golden Horn, up the Bosporus to the Black Sea and then by air-conditioned motor coach back to the Hilton. Assemble 9.30 a.m. sharp. We assembled, the eight Germans and I. I thought at first I was on the German Tour. The Turkish guide looked dapper from ten feet, but fell to pieces closer up, everything seemed to hang from his haggard moustache. At 9.25 a German asked if it was alright for us to board the motor coach waiting outside. The guide tapped his watch and said, 'My dear friends, 9.30 boarding of the motor coach.' At 9.30 we surged out of the lobby and into the motor coach, scrambling for the best seats. Here the guide addressed us in English and asked if we all spoke English. I nodded, as the only obvious English speaker, and the Germans grumbled and made noises meaning that they could if they had to.

'My dear friends, do you wish to return by the mountains or do you wish to return by the coast?' We were still seated outside the Hilton. How, I thought, do we answer that when, presumably, we hadn't seen the mountains or the coast (unless that was Tour A which maybe I should have taken as a pre requisite course).

'The coast,' said a 30-year-old German in an alpine wind jacket, 'definitely the coast.'

This German turned to another German, an old man in a dark, crumpled suit, bow tie, with a benign smile and a JAL bag slung in front of him like a bus conductor, 'what do you think professor – the coast yes?'

We all looked to the professor, maybe he was an expert in Byzantine art. He motioned with his hand and said, 'Of no consequence.' I warmed to him, he seemed to have a proper life attitude – that all destinies are equally interesting for those who live them out. We still hadn't moved from the front of the Hilton.

'My dear friends, the mountains or the coast?' the guide asked again. 'The mountains, I recommend the mountains.'

'The coast, there is nothing in the mountains,' said the alpine-jacketed German.

'The mountains,' I said for no reason.

'Well the mountains then it is,' the guide announced. We used to call that the forced card trick.

The German moved grumpily in his seat and the Hilton motor coach moved off to the Golden Horn.

'My dear friend,' the guide said to me, 'where are you from?'

'Australia.'

'Ah Australia! And which city?'

'Sydney.'

At this, the German in the alpine jacket broke in with a snort, 'Sydney, they all come from Sydney – there is no other city,' and was hugely amused by this observation.

'There is Melbourne,' the guide said with authority, looking at me.

'Yes, there is Melbourne,' I confirmed.

At the Golden Horn we would board the Hilton motor launch which I pictured of course, with deck tables, Cinzano umbrellas and white-coated waiters. Maybe deck quoits. Toss down a raki or two. But the tour guide seemed to have economised and bought instead nine tickets for the regular ferry run. A Manly-ferry-sized craft with goats, soldiers, peasants, and Turkish girls in the national costume of Wrangler jeans and Frye boots.

We set off up the Bosporus after scrambling for the best seats. The guide pointed out the occasional 'landmark' and the German in the alpine jacket began cracking the whip over the guide – extracting from him an excessive clarity of performance, not, it seemed, for his, the German's sake, but for the benefit of the rest of us. The guide, I must say, came out with some details which were close to the extraneous.

'My dear friends, this is the hotel for soldiers.'

'Hotel for soldiers?' prodded the German, 'for all soldiers?'

'No, for the officers.'

'For officers then of all countries and all armies?'

'No, only Turkish officers.'

'A barracks then?'

'No not a barracks, out of the barracks.'

'For this they pay nothing?'

'They pay but only not so much.'

I felt like saying enough, enough about the officers' hotel which was now two kilometres back.

Tour B up the Bosporus gained by not being thoroughly guided. I was certainly glad we did not have a German guide.

Yes, there was an old man on the ferry using his time to weave a fishing net. Yes, there were cadet officers of about twelve, in military uniform, crew cuts, peak caps, yellow lanyards, identical attaché cases and gloves held correctly in the other hand, going home on Sunday leave to eat lunch with parents in villages along the Bosporus.

Yes, they did drink cay (tea) in glasses brought by a boy with a swinging tray suspended from his hand, and they did eat yooort (yoghurt). Yes, they were cooking fish over coals in their small boats at the villages where we stopped and selling the cooked fish in buns. There were seaside restaurants in the sparkling sun of the Bosporus, where I would dearly have loved to have been, but Tour B was a no-lunch-included tour.

'My dear friends, that is the Focar – a good restaurant,' said the guide, pointing to one of the seaside places.

'To my taste,' said the alpine-jacketed German, 'the Cafe Bohemia is better, but check and double check the bill.'

Both restaurants, I point out, are Italian.

'How do you say that?' one of the note-taking Germans asked the guide.

'Focar, Focar,' said the guide.

The guide offered to take photographs for any of us who wished to pose. The professor was the only one who had his photograph taken, JAL bag included, and I thought I detected a touch of self-parody.

'The cakes, the trolley cakes,' a German suddenly asked, 'are they fresh at these places mentioned, sometimes the cakes are from yesterday.'

The alpine-jacketed German advised caution, yes always check the cakes.

I suppose by poking at them with a big German finger.

The Tour B up the Bosporus climaxed with the guide pointing into the misty distance and saying 'Black Sea, there is the Black Sea.'

We all looked. I could not see the Black Sea.

We were standing now on the wharf at Sariyer when the tour guide said with a groan, 'The short fat man! Where is the short fat man?'

We looked to the ferry pulling out from the wharf.

'He is missing,' the tour guide groaned, and rushed to the wharf edge. We all rushed with him and stood looking at the receding ferry.

We had lost a comrade in arms, a dear friend.

'Too bad for him,' the German in the alpine jacket said heartlessly.

Another German came forward and said, 'I am the short fat man.'

'No,' said the anguished guide, 'it is another short fat man.'

'No,' said the German, helpfully, '*I* am the short fat man.'

The tour guide shook his head.

I guessed that the loss of a member of a Hilton lobby tour, a dear friend, on the Black Sea is a disaster for a tour guide – he probably had an extended family to keep.

The German in the alpine jacket said, 'Name tags we should have.'

The tour guide said something in Turkish which roughly translated meant, 'Allah let this day end.'

We stood glumly on the wharf, but then the guide's face brightened, 'No, it is alright, the short fat man is from last night, Istanbul night-Life, my dear friends, it is alright, we are nine.'

There were smiles all round and we returned to our tour gaiety, limited as it was.

We joined a different vehicle, not an air-conditioned coach, but a ramshackle taxi bus with a curtain fringe along the front windscreen. We had to crowd into it. Obviously owned by a relative of the guide.

In the trip back over the mountains the Germans' minds turned to food.

They asked the guide whether the Bosporus Coffee Inn at the Hilton would be open. He did not know, which initiated a debate about it.

'The Rotisserie would not be open for sure,' said one.

'Not the Rotisserie but maybe the Coffee Inn or Pilsen Bar, they would be open.'

'Only light snacks available,' another speculated.

No cake trolley.

We stopped then some blocks from the Hilton and to our surprise were asked to leave the taxi bus.

'But this is not the Hilton,' the Germans said with some alarm.

The guide said, 'This taxi is not permitted to drive to the Hilton, but it is within walking distance and I will take you, dear friends, past the night club district.'

The Germans rose in complaint, 'But why is this?'

'Polis,' the guide said, unconvincingly, 'regulation.'

'That is not possible,' grumbled the Germans and muttered about the Bosporus Coffee Inn closing.

I announced that I was leaving the tour and would say goodbye.

The guide's face fell, 'My dear friend, the tour ends at the Hilton,' he said resignedly taking my hand, holding it overlong in the Turkish way. 'No thanks,' I said. I would walk about.

They all stood looking at me accusingly as I plunged into the seething street.

They probably discussed me as they trudged back to the Hilton led by the guide – probably branded me as a traitor to Tour B.

A newspaper could well have a Hilton correspondent to

report on the teeming life within international Hiltons, that one long foyer which stretches around the world.

It occurs to me, too, that Hiltons are like modern Crusader forts – they are fortresses for Western tourists surrounded by security and, here in Cairo, by Tourist Police.

One day people will visit the ruins of Hiltons.

Autobahnia
....

Well, Chief, this is Francois Blase calling in from abroad – taking the pulse of the world. As you know I'm not what you'd call God's great traveller. For one thing I travel too heavy because I need a lot of my things around me. I'd like to see the cabin trunk come back. And I stay at Hiltons instead of at dirt-cheap, authentic little hotels where you eat with the family. I'm happy to report that Hiltons haven't changed although an Indian who lives in Hiltons said that the Cairo Hilton had become 'a bit of a bazaar'. I'll check that out. But Hiltons are one of the familiar things I like to have around me.

You'll remember that on my last trip I discovered that Hiltonia was a secret country. This time my biggest joy has been discovering the secret country of Autobahnia. Autobahns, like the Hiltons, are a whole way of life.

I've always preferred the interval to the opera. I like Conference-ville – another secret country – because they're a reason for having all-night parties in college rooms. I like foreign countries because they give me a reason for sitting in an aircraft for many hours drinking, eating, reading, listening to music, yarning to the pilot in the cockpit and being a smart alec with the hostesses.

Foreign countries give me an excuse for visiting Hiltonia. Now for the autobahns.

Firstly, you have a choice of three lanes – the slow lane, the middle of the road and the fast lane. Naturally, I'm a fast-lane person. The middle lane is for worms and the slow lane is the one you take when you drop back to 100 km/h to read a map or take something out of your bag or change your sweater.

Then there are the *places de servicio*. Many options here. You can take just toilets and petrol or you can take toilets-telephone-petrol or toilets-telephone-petrol-snacks or you can go the whole way and take toilets-petrol-telephone-snacks-cafeteria-restaurant-bar-nursery-boutique-*farmacia*-information-money exchange-television-motel. And the land of Autobahnia is timeless – these places are always open. There are three classes of restaurant and I find the most expensive ones are the most chatty.

The rich talk to each other more. I think they're lonelier. You can sit around at a service stop over a beer talking about the dollar rate, the price of petrol a litre, the good Hiltons and not so good Hiltons.

The riff-raff *pique-nique* outside the restaurants and play with their engines and can be quite colourful. Autobahnia food is like airline food which I always enjoy in that it 'suggests' a nationality, but is vague enough for there not to be any problem about what you eat first. There are no gymnasia on the autobahns that I could find. I'll write to the *comité d' autoroute* about it.

But the urge to be back in the fast lane soon gets to you and you leave a half-finished beer, jump into your rented Mercedes and tool along the autopista or whatever at your 160 km/h upwards.

Here's a tip. You can tell what country you're in by whether it's called autobahn, autoroute, autopista or autostrada. If it's called Cahill Expressway you're home. The music on the radio is always Abba, or a homage to John Lennon, but the voices around it change.

At first I took notice of the signs which said *curiosité* and I'd stop and dutifully look at the ruin, monument or whatever. Then I realised that the signs were enough – that the signs have a little drawing of a ruin, or a castle, or a cathedral, or a spa, or a *museo d'art*. So when I saw these little drawings I'd pull over into the slow lane, drop down to a 100 ks and read my Baedeker's guide. That's enough.

And then I'd be back in the fast lane again, pushing dopes off into the middle by roaring up behind them flashing my headlights in the European manner.

Autobahns talk to you, they have their own little language, I can now talk autobahn German, autoroute French, autopista Spanish. I can read the altitude in three languages. There are about 300 different signs, more in Germany. There are more signs in Germany than you can ever hope to read at 160 km/h.

The *peage* or toll can get heavy, especially in France. You have to pull into the slow lane, drop back to 100 and scrabble about on the floor of the car, firstly for the currency of the country and then for the correct amount.

You need the correct amount for the *automatique* toll basket. The manual payment lane is for trucks, caravans and worms – too slow. So I tool into the *automatique* at 100 and hurl my money into the basket. If it's not the correct amount, or if you've hurled in Belgian francs instead of French francs, it screams in pain and a big fist comes out and biffs you on the nose. Or a hook shoots out and tears your rear bumper bar off. So get it right.

Hitchhikers work out of the *places de servicio* and sometimes they themselves will do you a *servicio*. You never know your luck on a strange autobahn. I had a dreadful argument with a

Belgian physicist who was hitching. I said I would only pick up
hitchhikers who spoke English.

I said nothing made the kilos go slower than sitting beside
some dope who couldn't speak English. Talking by sign
language is hard at 160 ks. He said this was unethical. You had
to take them regardless of language. I said they should have a
sign around their necks saying what language they spoke as
well as the one they usually have saying what city they're going
to. I'll write to the *comité d' autoroute* about it. As a matter of fact
I wouldn't mind being on the *comité d' autoroute*. I have a
number of ideas.

You fall in love on the autobahns too. If you sit behind
someone in the fast lane – someone who has your speed – and
together you force dopes over into the middle lane and you pass
through a couple of small countries together at 160-170-
180 km/h you find that you inevitably fall in love. Remember
at primary school you fell in love with the back of the head of
the girl in the desk in front of you. Those plaits, the beautifully
brushed and parted hair, the clean white blouse and pressed
tunic smelling of Murlex cleaner, the virginal neck.

Where was I? Oh yes, well it happens on the autobahn too:
you fall in love with the back of a head. Although in
Autobahnia the language of cars has developed a long way,
especially on the autopista of Spain. There they use right and
left blinkers, headlights, hazard lights, engine revving, the
horn – bips, half horn, full horn, held horn – and gestures,
usually to abuse or instruct dopes and worms. Well, soon it will
be possible to use car language to say 'I'm madly attracted to
you. Do you read Proust? Meet me at the next top-of-the -
range restaurant-bar *place de servicio* which takes American
Express.'

It's the same as passing a note in class. I tried this with a
combination of signals and mime including using the palms of
my hands to say: 'Do you read books?' But I never quite got

through. Remember that they have to read this through their rear vision mirror at 160 ks or whatever. Then they have to signal back 'Yes, I'd like a cocktail, I do read books and you drive with much *machismo*.' I'm sure it can be done. This is something the *comité d' autoroute* could tackle.

I'd like to write a novel about a couple who fall in love in the fast lane of an autobahn. They get to say 'I love you' with their blinkers and maybe the hazard light would have to be used as well. They get to know each other over cocktails at the *place de servicio,* make love for the first time at a P-Stop, get married at an historical cathedral (or maybe just at the sign), have their honeymoon at an autobahn motel or at a *playa de veraneo* resort just off an autobahn, their kids grow up in the autobahn nurseries – play with the other autobahn kids in the *place de servicio* lidos.

Well I'm writing this in the slow lane at about 100 ks but I've got to get moving. I'm off up the *route principia* to Jerusalem to eat at the restaurant Jesus used to eat at. Cheers.

Hi Chief,

Why did I choose Switzerland for my vacation? The Swiss believe they can survive a nuclear war. I like that kind of positive, forward thinking. Also you get more Benedictine abbeys per kilometre in Switzerland, according to the Michelin Green Guide. J-O-K-E. I don't go in for gothic cathedrals and Benedictine abbeys as much as I did once.

I really went to Switzerland because the swizzlestick was invented there and I'm something of a cocktail-bar cowboy as well as a nightclub roundsman. It comes from the slurring of the word 'switzer', the old word for a Swiss. Unfortunately the Swizzlestick Museum was closed.

But also being something of a bushman I did go to the Festival of the Swiss Army Knives. The Festival is held in the village of Zug where the men and women from the village wear giant replicas of the thirty or so different types of Swiss army knife, made from wood, aluminium, plastic. Actually, the knives now aren't so much 'army' – it's more the Swiss civilian knife. There is a knife for every purpose: the fisherman's knife, the camper's knife, the waiter's knife, the sailor's knife and so on. There is even a Princess's knife. Well, the people of the village dress up as a knife with their blades and tools and cork screws sticking out and all with distinctive caps or clothing denoting their function as a knife. So the villagers who come as the waiter's knife have trays and a napkin over their arms, as well as being inside the knife replica. With their blades and tools sticking out they look like a procession of hedgehogs. The other villagers come in costume as the objects of the knives' desires, so as to speak, dressed as corks, bottle tops, fish, cans, tomatoes. There were also two or three village humourists who came as cut fingers. One had a large replica of a Band-aid around the replica of the cut finger. One had a device which oozed stage blood. The cut fingers received loud applause from the spectators. Then followed nice folk dances and songs including the famous Dance of the Swiss Knives and it's all rather wonderful.

After the parade and the dancing in the village square there is a feast with the usual barrels of beer and casks of wine. By nightfall the knives have got a little drunk and begin chasing the bottle tops, corks and cans and so on. There are some real cut fingers, even cut throats, later in the night.

They have a regional expression, 'as mad as a cut Zug'. I left. I'd been drinking with the lady's purse knife and it was becoming a little dangerous.

At the Festival it is possible to order a custom-made knife. I, of course, did just that. They measure your fingers and palm of your hand so that the knife they make fits well into the hand and has the correct balance. You select which tools you want to have on the knife. I'm having mine made with hollow handles which can be filled with cognac and with two small cups which screw into one end. At the other end there will be a small peanut dispenser. The knife also has an electronic calculator which tells you what to tip in which country for which products and services (and a long, pointed flick blade for bell captains who think they haven't been tipped enough). The people from Victorinox – one of the companies which make the Swiss Army Knives – are going to call it the Blase Disconsolate Traveller's Knife.

HARD WORK DISPLAY

In Lucerne I went to the Hard Work Display (Arbeit Macht Frei). The Swiss are very good workers and proud of it and at the display they demonstrate some of the ancient skills and practices of hard work, showing children what it was like to work hard in the olden days before morning and afternoon breaks, the three-hour lunch, cigarettes, lavatories, and personal telephone calls. They showed someone answering the telephone before it had rung thirty or forty times which I found truly amazing. I hadn't seen that done for a long time. There was an automated model of a shop assistant who, when you activated the display by pushing the button, used the quaint old expression, 'No problems – we'll do that for you while you wait', which I hadn't heard for some years. Some of the children visiting the display were disbelieving. There was also an office without a clock where the workers began work at sunrise and stopped at sunset and automated models of employees who went to the washrooms to get ready to leave *after* the finishing time. Some of the countries where these practices have disappeared organise bus tours to the display. There are other things like specimen jars of sweat. I recommend the display to Australians visiting Europe but I have to warn that it's fairly exhausting.

MEDIEVAL WATCH TOWERS ARE GOOD VALUE

So far the best travel tip in Switzerland – for guys with tastes like mine, anyhow – are the medieval watch towers. You

know, they built them in towns and villages to look out over
the countryside for many kilometres to watch for the arrival of
tourist carriages so that the townspeople could prepare for yet
another bunch of weary travellers unfamiliar with the currency,
and hence the olde travellers' expression 'they saw you
coming'. Well, my advice is to find one of these towers – every
olde town has one – and climb (good exercise) the 100 metres
or so up the narrow spiral inner staircases, but do this at 10 a.m.
or 2 p.m. on a weekday during school term – avoid the school
vacation. At about this time you have a very good chance that a
bus load or two of school girls will arrive and begin filing up
the narrow stair case. You can then begin your descent. Not to
everyone's taste, perhaps, but it gave me a buzz. Frankly, it was
the highlight of the trip. More fun than being chased by a
drunken Swiss army knife.

MICHELIN GUIDE INSPECTORS' CONFERENCE

In Geneva I was fortunate to come in on the last few days of the
Michelin Inspectors' Conference. They were arguing over
revisions to new editions of the guides. There were those who
argued against the emphasis on abbeys and cathedrals and who
wanted more battle fields and bullet-riddled, blood-stained
uniforms of archdukes.

Readers will be interested to know that the Michelin Working Party on Australia again decided not to put out a Michelin
Guide to Australia because there were insufficient Benedictine
abbeys and crusader castles and no blood-stained uniforms of
archdukes available in Australia to fill a Michelin Guide. The
Aboriginal people have a lot to answer for – having failed to
construct one single crusader fort or gothic cathedral in the
50 000 years they have allegedly been in the country. The
Michelin people were absolutely bewildered about the fact that

the Aboriginal people haven't got one ruin. I suppose they could begin making some. That't not a bad idea.

FINISHING SCHOOL FOR UNFINISHED PEOPLE

There's now a Swiss Finishing School in Geneva for mature-aged people who haven't quite matured. It's for people who were late getting started with life. There are courses for people who were too busy to learn the art of living or didn't have the right upbringing. People like me who grew up in a shoe box. There's a special intensive course for people who simply aren't very good at living. It teaches you things like how to use a bidet, how to play roulette, the firm handling of bell captains, how to win at poker games played on trains.

THE FREE DRUGS TRIP

My other Swiss experience was a factory tour of Roche, the drug manufacturer. You are given a fascinating sample kit of their drugs to take away with you. And you get to sample all sorts of mood changing chemicals. You can volunteer to join their drug trials program and get free courses of experimental drugs and at the same time participate in the advancement of medicine. I volunteered for the traveller's drug trial. Roche are developing a drug which purifies water, neutralises harmful bacteria in food, lowers Traveller Paranoia, suppresses anxiety, releases energy, clarifies the mind, inhibits flight dysrhythmia, stops diarrhoea, prevents foot ache in art galleries, and gives the traveller a stable sense of euphoria and confidence, exuding at the same time an aura which repells bores and malaria-carrying mosquitoes and attracts interesting, influential English-speaking nationals in bars.

Of course, the drug is in its early developmental stage. They hope though to get it together in one tablet taken daily. I've begun the trial and will let readers know my reports to Roche over the following year. I'll let you Roche my readers . . . I'll effect my Roche tests on the readers . . . I'll . . .

CULTURAL DELEGATE
....

As a cultural delegate, Blase tried always to read the protocol guides to the sensitivities and customs of other nationalities. Although he knew in his heart that he was a bad cultural delegate he did, at least, worry about protocol.

He knew, for instance, that the Chinese were punctual and took speech-making and banqueting seriously. This pleased Blase, himself no mean banqueter back home and also known as something of a speech-maker. He knew that the Chinese did not dress formally and Blase decided to confine himself to an elegantly-tailored Mao jacket and cap from Bucks of Melbourne.

He knew that, when the Chinese clap you, you are expected to clap them in return. With the Chinese you avoided excessive physical contact and boisterous behaviour. He knew about giving gifts to institutions and not to individuals and that expensive gifts such as automobiles and computers were embarrassing to the Chinese (advice which came as a relief to Blase, who liked to travel 'heavy', but not that heavy).

He knew not to tip and he knew not to give the Chinese nicknames. He knew not to display affection publicly and not to show anger either to other members of the delegation or towards the Chinese. There were to be no punch-ups. He knew there was also to be no public drunkenness and that the Chinese were moralistic about sex. And guests leave banquets ten minutes after the hot towels.

So although he was no good at inspecting things, could not remain attentive and questioning for long periods and had no interest in magnificent scenery, Blase at least knew his protocol.

Consequently, Blase went to his first banquet in his elegant Mao jacket and cap and with a pocketful of cheap kangaroo pins and was devastated when the Chinese turned up in dinner suits. They were also a bit drunk, slapped everyone on the back, threw food at each other, kissed him on the mouth, grabbed his genitals at every occasion and asked not too subtly for gifts, including automobiles and motorbikes.

He was offered sex, and the party did not stop ten minutes after the hot towels, but went on into the early hours. Later they all crept into an army barracks and stole a People's Liberation Army flag.

Next day in the bar of the Jing Jiang Club, recovering from his hangover, Blase, in his food-stained Mao jacket and cap, asked his Guide what had gone wrong. Blase had a profound sense of cultural confusion. The Guide was still drunk and they had shaken off the rest of the delegation, who were wandering lost in the alleys of Shanghai.

At first the Guide wouldn't explain, but after being given a Chinese burn he revealed that the Chinese, too, had been briefed on protocol for handling Australians. The Guide gave Blase a translation.

Australians are easy-going about time and punctuality and consider it over-conscientious to be on time. To be late is to protest against despotic employers.

Australian men like to dress up in dinner suits as a way of aping their former aristocratic rulers. Australians enjoy physical contact and there are hotels in Australian cities where men go to kiss other men and hold hands; likewise women. This is becoming the custom.

Australians like to tip and give gifts as a way of showing their generosity, as a way of rewarding good service and as a way of aiding poor nations.

Australians like to break time-honoured rules and customs as a way of showing their independence from the chains of the past – for example, climbing to the top of a sacred monument and placing a beer can there, stealing a Chinese flag from an army barracks, diving into ponds and trying to catch century-old goldfish. This is called Larri-kin-ism.

Australians are accustomed to indulging their sexual appetites at every available opportunity, especially while travelling in other countries, which is considered to be a 'holiday from marriage'. Singsong girls should be found for Australian males and Chinese studs for Australian women.

Australians like to make jokes at each other which is called 'taking the mick-ie'. Australian men sometimes grab each other's genitals as a gesture of comradeship known as Goo-sing.

Australian women like to take off their tops at every opportunity for sunbathing and prefer not to wear bras. But Chinese men should practise the Three Nos laid down by the last People's Congress – 'No staring, No touching and No funny business'.

Australian language is rich in animal imagery and so they say horsing around, goo-sing, snake in the pocket, no bull-defecation and they like to go on what they call pussy hunts. Australians become angry if they think that a person is bull-defecating.

Australians are artistic people who sometimes build elaborate sculptures from beer bottles or beer cans while drinking. They will sometimes take the Guide's hat and throw it around, one to the other, but this must be seen as a need to release excess energy from a high protein diet and short working week.

Australian men are also forever fly-checking. This is not a sexual gesture but an old horse-riding custom to reassure themselves that no injury has befallen that part.

Australian men may be observed smelling bicycle seats because, as a nation of horsemen (see film, *The Man from Snowy River*), the smell of the bicycle seat reminds them of the saddle of the horse back home which they miss.

Souveniring: Australians come from a penal colony and, as a remembrance of their ancestors, still like to practise 'symbolic theft' as a gesture against the rich. They will often take things they do not need from a public place; for example, you may see them trying to take a park bench home. Pay no heed.

When doing business with Australians, Chinese should beware of the saying, 'I'll toss you double or nothing'.

Beware of such Australian expressions as 'Let's talk about it over lunch' (they will try to get you drunk), 'Let's leave the details to the accountants', 'Of course there is a little something in it for you', 'We don't want the taxman getting his hungry little hands on any of it', 'I don't think there's any need to put that in writing', 'One for you, one for me and one for the family trust', 'I have a little off-shore company that handles those problems', 'Something's come a little unstuck but it's all under control – my MD does what I tell him', 'We're in a grey area but that's my reading of the investment guidelines – let's give it a punt', and 'We'll handle the documentation at our end if you like'.

Never do business with an Australian who says 'no worries' a lot.

That the Chinese knew so much about the Australian soul plunged Blase into deep gloom and he and the Guide stayed in the Jing Jiang Club for two days playing billiards with the New Zealand Female Steeple-Jumping Delegation.

The members of the delegation feel that Francois Blase should not be a cultural delegate in future. Or, in fact, represent his country in any capacity.

While abroad, he mopes in his room too much. He is apathetic about scenery. He does not seem to know what to say about scenery. He sometimes refuses to look at it. He says it makes him 'ineffably sad'.

He does not know the words of Waltzing Matilda. He is uncertain about how much iron ore Australia produced last year. He often will not come out of his room despite efforts by the Leader of the Delegation and the Guide. He pretends to be ill.

He refused to go into an ancient Buddhist temple built without the use of nails 'Because,' he said, 'if a Buddhist temple is going to fall, it will be me it falls on.' Sometimes he refuses to leave the car saying that he 'will watch from the window'. While the rest of the delegation goes inspecting, he drinks beer with the driver and listens to the car radio.

When our hosts ask the delegation what it is they would like to see, Blase says 'anything with blood on it'. He asks to be taken to war museums and museums of the people's uprising, knowing full well that cultural delegations are about peace and friendship and not about how many rounds a minute the AK-47 fires.

He spends days at a time in the Jing Jiang Club and such places with the New Zealand Female Steeple-Jumping Delegation. He does Chinese breathing exercises to the embarrassment of his hosts. He smuggles things in and out of countries using his Official Passport. Some days he asks no questions. He hums the song 'Moon River' to annoy the rest of the delegation. He seems morbidly interested in starvation and infant mortality.

He embarrasses the Guide by asking all the time about what

he calls 'jig jig'. He makes long speeches at the banquets out of turn and alludes to 'dark things of the soul'. At the performance of *The Official and His Five Daughters* by the all-female cast of the Hangzhou Opera Company, he went backstage and pursued the juvenile lead and persisted in inviting her back to the hotel for 'supper'.

In Shanghai he invited the Jolly Cooks and the Jumps From the Spring Board Performers back to the hotel after the acrobatics and we've heard that the Jolly Cooks did not appear the following night (the first performance they've missed since the troupe was formed twelve years ago). They kept the whole hotel awake singing 'Moon River'.

On the train trip to Guiling he took out a pack of cards and went 'looking for some action'. We did not see him for sixteen hours and we heard that he taught poker to the attendants and won from them the equivalent of their year's wages. When we remonstrated with him about this he said: 'That's what I call cultural exchange.'

His business card is supposed to be 'amusing' but leaves much to be desired in the area of good taste. Loosely translated, it says something like 'Master of Jig Jig'.

Enclosed is a recording of a 'cultural exchange' Blase had with a Mr Cao in Beijing which we submit as supporting evidence:

'Tell me, Mr Cao, in our country we have a saying that the hunter must know the animal he stalks. Do you think that is the purpose of cultural exchange? Is that what our leaders have in mind?'

The Guide translates. Mr Cao laughs and then replies in Chinese.

Guide: Mr Cao says yes, we too hunt in the outer provinces. The peasants hunt for hare.

Blase: I do some hunting myself. Do you need a licence to own a gun in China?

Mr Cao laughs and replies.

Guide: Mr Cao says that in our country we have a saying: 'The
    dogs bark, the caravan moves on.' Do you have such a
    saying?
Blase: We say that the dog that does not bark may still bite. I see
    very few dogs in your country. I believe they are eaten.
    The Guide translates. Mr Cao laughs and replies.
Guide: Mr Cao says that in your country he believes dogs are
    raced for amusement.
Blase: Does Mr Cao eat dogs?
    The Guide translates. Mr Cao laughs and replies.
Guide: Mr Cao says it is too early to eat, but if you are hungry
    he will buy an ice on the stick. Do you have ice on the stick in
    your country?
Blase: We have 200 varieties of ice on the stick, including one
    called Dracula's Blood.
    The Guide translates. Mr Cao laughs and replies.
Guide: Mr Cao says we have a folk tale called the Ice Fairy in
    which a young man falls in love with a beautiful woman, not
    knowing that she is made of ice. In the spring . . . But it is a
    long story and a sad story. We do not have time.
Blase: We have women made of ice in our country.
    The Guide translates. Mr Cao laughs and replies.
Guide: Mr Cao is surprised you have ice in your country. We
    believe it to be desert.
Blase: We have mountains on the coast. But there is much
    desert and it could not not support a large population – if a
    large population suddenly were to come there. What calibre
    shot gun does Mr Cao have?
    The Guide translates. Mr Cao laughs and replies.
Guide: Mr Cao says he owns a 12-gauge Winchester over and
    under. He says why don't we stop this faeces about folk tales
    and iron ore production and grab a couple of dozen cold cans
        and go shoot everything that moves in the forest.
Blase: Tell Mr Cao that suits me fine.
    Mr Blase and Mr Cao then left the party and refused to rejoin

it for the completion of the day's itinerary. They allegedly shot beer cans in the Forest of International Harmony.

We recommend that Francois Blase not represent Australia on any further delegations. If the Department receives letters approving of Mr Blase from Mr Cao, the Jolly Cooks, the Jumps From the Spring Board Performers or the juvenile lead of the Hangzhou Opera, we suggest they be evaluated in the light of this report.

(signed) Leader of the Delegation

I met the Systematic Traveller in the bar of the Holiday Inn in Albuquerque.

I'd been there for a day or so, in the bar.

'These things are essential, Blase,' he said, 'inanimate experience in the mornings – museums and monuments – where you don't have to deal with people and when there is little crowd at things. Never call up people in the morning – no one likes a stranger in the morning.'

It was certainly true sexually.

'I'll give you a tip, Blase – the famous are often lonely. It doesn't hurt to give them a call.'

I told him my travel problem was getting out of bed in the motel in the morning. I dread the cleaning staff and they dread me. I sometimes stayed most of the morning in those abundant, dial-control American showers. Getting by the bell captain who felt he'd been insufficiently tipped, too, was a problem.

I said I did a lot of my travelling in the bar watching colour TV and talking to the barmen.

The Systematic Traveller shook his head sadly.

'I classify all conversations into three categories,' the S.T.

told me, 'casual – up to fifteen minutes – extended, and depth-interviews which I record and transcribe. But I also record and summarise the other conversations – and overheard conversations. I cut things from local publications which illustrate the character of the place, I collect posters, advertising slogans, slang words, transit tickets, labels, empty product packets. I photograph characteristic architecture both commercial and domestic, I do shop fronts, street signs – I search out other statistics like ethnic groupings and I do a chart – history of the city with dates and events from other places – to put it in a world perspective. I have a gastronomic section where regional foods and wines I've tried are listed with my comments – wines and ales.'

I sat hunched, wordless, sulky, hostile, defiant and inadequate.

'It's really a personal graph of my mood as well as anything else – I see travel as a way of moving 'me' as a sensor, through a set of experiences. I create a Gestalt from all the scattered input.'

He noticed my silence. 'But anyhow Blase – you've travelled – what's your personal method?'

'I have talked with many bell captains – I took one to the District Court of New York.'

'Taxi drivers, barmen (he dropped his voice) I call them "responders" – they tell you what you want to hear – they deal professionally with strangers – no I avoid them – at all costs – very distorting.'

'Another?' I asked, touching our beer glasses.

'Yes, thank you, but not the same brand. Just to illustrate my system – I always drink something different. Rarely do I taste the same thing twice. I notice you're drinking Heineken – a Dutch beer – a very good beer – but here in Albuquerque?! Wrong move. Always try the product of the region.'

I stubbornly ordered another Heineken and he had Beer X (sample 1). 'I drink Heineken because I can find it anywhere in the world and it's a familiar thing in an unfamiliar environment.'

I could see he was unimpressed with this.

'But,' I said, 'you see, I place much emphasis on recording and observing the stress which travel brings to bear on my system. And on passive absorption of street and bar ambience. Anything that happens to you is "experience". You on the other hand insert yourself too aggressively into the experience. You are too strong a chemical in the mixture.'

He was taken aback, but did not seem to place much value on my opinion.

I went on, 'I consider travel a random, worthless, and unnatural experience. Maybe one of those unnecessary activities imposed by boredom and status and affluence on people like us. A custom. Unless you have a specialised interest in churchyards and gravestones,' I said, recalling my English experience.

'I simply can't agree,' he said, drinking Beer X with some agitation.

But I was well underway. 'At least one-third of travel is *learning how to travel*, which is completely inapplicable to your normal life when you return home. There is then the negative experience of looking in the rear-vision mirror of your life – and you learn by travelling just how anxious, alone and defenceless you are. Who wants to learn that? Travel is for me incapacitation and disorientation. I think that at first I hoped that travel would chase away the overcast cloudiness of my own personal preoccupation. Instead, I found that I was deeper into preoccupation. Staying at home was more *distracting* in that sense. I usually find a *circle of self* inflates around me like a space suit, which prevents the experience from touching me. I bob along. Maybe in recollection – by story telling – the experience of travel comes alive. I find *essence* through repetition not from incessant newness.'

The bar had fallen silent. The other conversations had

ceased. The barman had paused in his polishing of the glasses to listen.

'But how do you get a picture of the places you've been to?' the S.T. said, harriedly.

'I don't,' I said glumly, 'I just don't. I can't generalise, that's my problem. I can't wrap up my observations in a dazzling conclusive verbal sachet. After all, travel is a damned expensive way to arrive at inconclusiveness. For instance, others can see clearly whether a country is "happy" or not. My parents, my brothers, my fellow travellers who sit beside me in airplanes, buses and so on, can readily tell if a country is "happy". Once, in Toronto, in the central business district, I tried to count the number of Canadians who were smiling in the street – if they were all Canadians – but I found too many suspect smiles. I had to keep discounting for professional smiles, the wheedling smiles of drunks, the tranced-out smiles of Hari Krishna beggars, courtesy smiles of motel clerks, the nervous smiles of chance eye-encounters in lifts. A lot of nervous smiles came from people who saw me looking into their faces, searchingly.

The S.T. said that he found the Italians were a race that was either 'laughing or crying.'

'That would be easier to observe and count, I suppose,' I said.

'They are also the most open people in the world.'

'You mean candid?' I queried, 'I have been told the Americans talk openly about their personalities and sex problems – at least on the West Coast, or more particularly, Los Angeles – or San Francisco – or maybe just the film people and those from Marin County.'

'Not like the Americans at all,' he said, grumpily, 'no, Italians are open in their feelings.'

'But not their personality problems?'

'They are a much simpler race than the Americans. More like the Balinese.'

I envied him. I wanted just once to return confident of what

I'd seen, to amuse those who cluster around you when you are the returned traveller.

'I know,' I exclaimed, 'I have met a lot of friendly liars in all nationalities. "Bullshitting" we Australians call it.'

But really, every time a generalisation begins to form in my mind a school of carp attack it and leave behind a ravaged, fleshless remark.

'Chileans are given to exaggeration,' I read, 'they are the kindest, most tolerant, humane people imaginable.' Just the idea of testing that generalisation made me feel tired; I felt defeated by the idea of setting up a way of testing it at all.

The barman joined in, 'But you can tell us something about your own people – what about the way they dress – Australians have a reputation of being rather careless in their dress.'

My face must have lit up with enthusiasm about the question – like all travellers, my opinion of my own people, information about my homeland, is eagerly at the service of all mankind. It is the most honourable of patriotisms.

'I once analysed twenty-four dress styles in Australia into which just about everyone fits, with some interesting exceptions which I'll point out later, but the styles are: elegant-expensive, flash-expensive, respectable-conservative, respectable-daring, cheap-conservative, cheap-flash, respectable-uncaring, cheap-uncaring, trendy-expensive, bohemian-trendy, bohemian-traditional, impoverished, derelict, uniformed civilian-traditional (butchers), uniformed civilian glamorous (rent-a-car staff), arty-sartorial, arty-inexpensive, arty-individual, rural-bourgeois, rural-worker, eccentric rich, eccentric-derelict.'

'Oh really?' the barman said, his interest dead.

I'm often asked too about street drunkenness in Australia and alcohol. I do know the figures on this – on numbers of arrests for drunkenness, alcohol-related crimes, variations within the States and between the States, committal figures for treatment of alcoholics, membership of AA, consumption-per-head, impressions of street intoxication city-by-city, sub-cultural customs.

No one had ever heard me through. Do they really want to know about alcohol and drunkenness in Australia or not?

I have always felt, though, that at least I should be able to' classify people of the world into rude, polite, friendly. Every other traveller can. I said that the English had not been patronising to me.

'Ah,' said the S.T., 'you have missed the subtlety of their rudeness. The British make an art of being rude in a way that you cannot detect.

'Well, that's fine by me,' I said, 'if I miss the concealed rudeness I take away only the impression of excessive politeness.'

Actually, I didn't tell them, but I am forced at times to invent generalisations so that I do not diminish the value of travel. I have to invent them at times to prove that I've actually been where I've said I've been.

But the truth of it is I rove the world in an inconclusive state. I am a very bad guest speaker on travel.

'Well,' the barman said, 'you'll not find a city soon – outside Australia – where it's safe for tourists.'

'The problem of mugging is as old as cities themselves, and can be solved,' I told them.

'Boswell complained of it in London in 1763. The answer is to wear a sword and carry a stout walnut stick. But I have historical figures on street crime ...'

The most practised Australian journalistic genre is the Letter from New York and I thought, Chief, that I should lay down some guidelines (with examples) for the younger members of staff.

It must begin with a quote from a New York cab driver. They are always so racy, pithy, hip, colourful, insightful, and they know who's going to win (anything). But I see that the *TWA Guide to New York* says, 'Don't be surprised if the New York taxi drivers do *not* regale you with disclosures on the city's labour problems or a critique of the current administration . . .' Evidently they are tired of being interviewed by Australian reporters (and academics doing an obligatory piece to qualify for a taxation deduction) who arrived at Kennedy Airport. Anyhow, I haven't found a driver who speaks complete English.

An insight into the colour question: In a Western Union office I was sending a telegram when a negro boy about 18, swaggered in and said in a loud voice to no one in particular, to us all in general, 'Ah is going home, I've had enough of this town. I'm telling my mama I'm coming home.' He took a pile of telegram forms and pen poised, turned to me and said, 'Say man, how you spell Detroit?' I told him. He wrote that down and then turned to me again, 'How you spell Michigan?' (Maybe that's a literacy-crisis item more than a colour-question item.)

Ain't-it-a-tough-city-incident: Being a warm-hearted and easy-going guy, at ease with the world, I began talking to a black whore in the Biltmore bar. I wasn't interested in doing business with her – I was there, wasn't I, to visit room 2109 where Scott and Zelda had their honeymoon – but nor, on the other hand, was I doing a reporter-who-pays-whore-for-interview-but-does-not-touch-her-story. We talked about the dreams we had for ourselves and our people. She told me how in the 1930s and 1940s coloured people couldn't kiss on stage or screen because it showed they had real human emotion. I said that in Australia men were still not allowed to kiss sheep on stage and screen. She said that she thought men were not allowed to kiss sheep on stage or screen even in New York! The conversation had that relaxing frankness you get with a stranger when you're feeling low and don't give a damn. However, I did keep an alert nerve near my wallet. She complimented me on my sensitivity to her race and to animals. We said goodnight (I was too tired). Back in my hotel room I found that while my wallet was still with me, my American Express card which I kept separately in another pocket was missing. She'd stolen it. Since then I've been told that stolen credit card are worth $500 on the street. I fell into a deep depression – travellers who lose their American Express card are like police officers who lose their guns.

Prostitutes have taken over the language of radical psycho-therapy and call whorehouses 'sensitivity centres' and the whores are called 'counsellors'. Seems reasonable to me.

How some things are universal and never changing even in New York: An 8-year-old negro boy in East Harlem to his friend: 'Why did the chicken cross the road?' The friend said, 'Because he saw your face.' The 8-year-old said, 'No, to get to the other side.'

A New York subway graffiti story: Young people still do elaborate illegal decoration of the subway trains with spray paint, although now art galleries and art groups take up the best and market their work. But my carriage was done through with 'Ricardo is finished with graffiti'.

A dinner party in Greenwich Village which sums it all up story: An academic lives with a woman who is a feminist psychotherapist. She runs a Women's Psychotherapy Referral Service – fifty psychotherapists who have been active in the women's movement and have participated in consciousness raising. At dinner they told me they were going to marry after having lived together, 'it is the most bohemian thing left to do in New York – getting married.' Someone at the dinner party asked the woman if she were going to invite her group therapy patients to the wedding. She laughed and said no, it was going to be a traditional family wedding 'with vows, the lot.'

Quaint ideas about Australia story: A drunken professor of music from Maryland asked me if I had ever screwed a sheep because he'd heard that a bit of that went on down under. I said it was interesting that he should mention that as I had heard a paper in Italy on just that subject. Oh really? he said. He said the thing that intrigued him was how you chose which one to screw when there were 53 million of them. I said that according to the paper it was like being in a lift, there is always one person in the lift you would go to bed with by the time it has reached your floor. But, he said, there was no communication, the sheep couldn't express *its* preferences. I said that speech was not the only band of communication. It was no different to making love with someone who couldn't speak English. He was satisfied by my answers. I said I'd send him a copy of the academic's paper from Italy. I always wanted to ask, he said. 'One day I'd like to visit Australia.'

What's happening in art (to show that painters are crazy and art no longer makes sense and why don't they get back to painting landscapes and horses): At the downtown Whitney, Agnes Denes has *An Exhibition of Human Dust*, photographic and mixed media. It includes bones, sperm and other human mong. That's called mixed media. In the same exhibition there was a space with the words 'withdrawn in protest'. The artist had entered a painting and withdrawn it because he was opposed to galleries. Another exhibit is about a hundred photographs of people cleaning and working in an office building (the building in fact, where the exhibition was) called, *I Make Maintenance Art One Hour Every Day*. The artist Merle Laderman Ukeles wrote to the people who cleaned the building and asked them to consider one hour of their day of regular work to be 'art'. The artist photographed them during one of these hours. Agnes Denes was lucky that her exhibit wasn't cleaned away during Merle Laderman Ukeles's project.

What's happening among the radicals: There are Demon Dances against the nuclear war. I call them demon dances because they often seem to involve coffins and death and skeletons.

There was a memorial service for the American socialist Eugene Victor Debs who ran for the presidency five times from 1912. He polled at best a million votes – about one-sixth of the votes cast then. He campaigned from jail once where he spent three years for opposing American participation in World War I. I have always liked his remark that people had to make socialism themselves. 'If I could lead you to socialism someone else could lead you out.' Three hundred old socialists attended the service.

What are the intellectuals talking about at parties: They talk about how great the 1960s were politically, how committed and alive politics was then. I suggested that they campaign to bring back the Vietnam War.

What is the newest current expression: 'When we come down to the wire.' No one knew where it came from. Maybe the wire is

the barbed wire which troops had to face in trench warfare.
There is a lot of talk about 'energy'. On my last trip energy
meant fuel and the world energy crisis. Now the word has
jumped across to mean 'creativity' as if the trauma of Americans
losing their fuel power, their automobiles, has continued as an
anxiety about their personal drive. So everyone wants to mix
with energised people, people are frightened about losing their
energy – vitamin taking began during the fuel crisis. People are
looking for 'energy foods'. People talk about places where the
energy is or isn't. Australia is where the energy is. The
Australian film industry is where the energy is. New viruses are
feared because they take away your energy. They talk of aerobic
energy (from food input) and an aerobic energy (from the
body's reserve).

What is the latest food fad: energy foods. Even chewing gum is
being advertised as giving 'a lift' i.e. in energy. I still use neat
Jack Daniels or a Stinger.

A New York Jewish story: One late-middle-age Jewish woman to
another, 'In Israel, tell me, how much to have your mouth
rehabilitated?' Before the other woman could answer, the New
York woman went on to say that in New York to have a 'mouth
survey', new teeth and 'general reconstructions' cost $5,000.
But New York is still a very conservative city: I couldn't get into
Regines, the discotheque, because I wasn't wearing a 'regular
jacket and tie'.

The obligatory piece on New York should also include a
Warm-hearted American People story, and a *Pithy New York
bartender remark* and *A piece on the Chrysler Building.*

BLASE AND DEEP TISSUE MASSAGE
AND OTHER FULFILMENT THERAPIES

Hi Chief. As you might have guessed, I'm hanging out in Sausalito with some lapsed radicals from the 1960s – the hometown of the California Hot-tub world, Sausalito in Marin County, overlooks foggy San Francisco bay. Marin has every sort of fulfilment therapy including heavy drinking.

My first experience of Marin County fulfilment therapy was Tracy, a cocktail waitress at No Names Bar where I hang out when I'm in Marin. Tracy understands the restless soul. In Marin they have a style of talking which is very mellow and a vocabulary which has no edges to it.

Tracy isn't really a cocktail waitress: she's a student seriously into deep-tissue massage therapy. She has been doing political science but moved across to physical therapy. In New York I found that the whores called themselves therapists, here in Marin the nice girls are into deep-tissue massage therapy (and all it can suggest).

'You are relating in a hands-on way to people and at least you see two years of tension roll away and people get up from the table smiling,' she said.

'With political science it's all verbalising and you never

know whether you're doing good or bad.'

Later we tooled up to Bolinas in her Mustang to Smiley's Bar which is an old hippy hangout.

When I walked into the bar I felt I'd walked back 10 years – more – it is the place where all the hippies and flower children came to die.

Now they play Space Invaders and pool.

The vegetarian cafe opposite Smiley's showed an uncharacteristic sense of humour for a vegetarian cafe and named itself Scowleys.

When I said to Tracy, 'My God, this is it – this is the bar where all the hippies and flower children come to die,' she became very upset.

'My step-father is an old hippy,' she said, 'and he's a very mellow kind of guy.'

'Don't get me wrong,' I said, 'I'm an old hippy myself. I wouldn't mind coming here to Bolinas and Smiley's bar to die.'

I said that we old hippies didn't seem to have left much of a mark on the world.

'I disagree strongly,' Tracy said, 'and it's all going to come back (please no!) and this time it is really going to be a revolution 'cause all the old hippies are in power places and things like that and they'll respond to new hippies.'

Well, maybe.

Tracy told me that Bolinas was where the 'whale thing began' where the Friends of the Earth headquarters were, and where Brautigan blew his brains out.

The dogs all have a dreadful flea problem and scratch themselves against buildings and on gravel roads because the people of Bolinas don't use flea wash or flea spray and rely instead on organic collars soaked in herbs. The dogs say it doesn't work.

There are no drug stores in Bolinas (in the accepted meaning of the word 'drug').

Marin has two great beach villages – Bolinas and Stinson

Beach. Stinson beach is more chic.

'Actually,' Tracy said, 'you should start your drinking at Stinson Beach – at the Sand Dollar bar – and finish the night at Smiley's – you have your first ten cocktails at the Sand Dollar and your second ten at Smiley's.

'You know what a cocktail dress is?' Tracy asked. 'Well, I'll tell you – it's a dress you need five cocktails before you are mellow enough to wear it'.

In the Sand Dollar we saw this really unhappy chic lady with her arm in a sling and both eyes black – really black – she seemed to have been in a bar brawl.

The cocktail waitress at the Sand Dollar told us the story.

This lady's husband had gone away for a week on business and for the first time in her life the lady decided to go to Bolinas and pick up a guy for the night. She had her ten cocktails at the Sand Dollar and tooled up to Smiley's in her BMW where she picked up an ex-hippy flower-power boy and took him home for the night. At home he bashed her up, set fire to the luxury beachside house, stole her BMW car and crashed it into the sea, where it still was.

The chic lady with her arm in the sling clutching her Tequila Mary heard the waitress telling us the story and called out – in the saddest voice I've heard – 'even here in Marin there will be some explaining to do when my man gets home tomorrow. Oh boy.'

Next day Tracy and I went over to the Berkeley campus where all the radicalism of the 1960s began and the inspiration of much that happened in radicalism in Australia. I explained to Tracy that we were part of it – even in Sydney – we knew all about the Free Speech movement and Mario Savio and the underground newspapers. She said that although she was too young to have been in it her stepfather had told her all about it.

I told her that in Sydney we pronounced it — 'Barkley' (as in 'Berkeley Square' in England) because we'd read about the Berkeley campus, but none of us had been there.

I didn't tell her that I'd also been a beatnik which also started in San Francisco – before she was born.

The Berkeley campus seems more into parachuting and windsurfing these days.

The *Berkeley Barb* newspaper no longer exists, but the campus newspaper, *The Daily Californian,* had a stale obligatory article by Noam Chomsky on plans he thought Israel had for controlling Jordan, Syria, Lebanon, Egypt and South Africa. But the big story in *The Daily Californian* was on the 'mellowing of rock and roll'. The page-one story was a round-up of the rock scene and especially the all-woman group the Go-Gos. 'Their music is fun (like Disneyland) and safe (like Suburbia).'

Just off campus Tracy took me to the People's Mural, which is painted along the building near the People's Park – the scene of many historic radical gatherings. The mural shows the history of radicalism from the 1960s to the 1980s – the free speech movement – anti-Vietnam War, flower power, psyche-delic drugs, environmentalists, commune movement, and finally the mural shows the People's Park as it is now – occupied by burned-out kids, alcoholics and beggars.

Tracy noticed some grafitti on the mural and exclaimed that until recently no one would have written graffitti on the People's Mural – 'That's a really tacky thing to do,' she said unhappily.

Everyone outside Marin County is reading *The G Spot and other recent discoveries about human sexuality,* by Alice Kahn Ladas, Beverly Whipple and John D. Perry .

In Marin, of course, they knew about the G spot years ago. It took a long time for some of us to learn about the other spot and now we have to worry about the G spot. The Grafenberg spot is a female pleasure source inside the vagina. Female ejaculation, is in too.

But seriously, Chief, there's a lot in the G spot thing – Tracy says it's true. When you touch it the woman says, 'Gee'.

I'll hang out a little longer at the No Names Bar awaiting the old telex saying, 'Extend indefinitely Marin County assignment. Send series on G spot, deep tissue massage, and the mellowing of rock and roll.'

BLASE IN PACIFIC PARADISE

The Editor, Dear sir, I am the Recreation Director of the Inter-Continental Hotel, Port Vila, Vanuatu. The well-being and harmony of the guests here at the Inter-Continental is my first concern. There is someone here called Francois Blase claiming to be a travel writer for your magazine and wanting 15 per cent off everything. He's been asking for special rates from the nautch girls at the Club Privé He did a performance which he called 'Somerset Maugham in Love' at the hotel talent quest on Monday and despite the fact that no one seemed to understand the act, he won the vote by rigging things with the staff and some air hostesses and won the lamp made from coral.

Here at the Inter-Continental we try to get people together for tennis and golf, and so on, and they can put their names on the guest notice board. This Blase has put up a sheet for polo and wants to get up a polo team to 'ride against' the White Sands Country Club. But it takes four people with three ponies each to play polo. We do not have horses here. The people who come to the Inter-Continental can't ride horses. This has caused consternation.

He says that one always plays polo in the cool of the

afternoon and it was always the highlight of his stay in India as a cultural delegate. Vanuatu in not India. He gets around in ridiculous gear from his days in Beirut which he gets from a company called Banana Republic Travel and Safari Clothing Company in Polk Street, San Francisco and of which he claims to be an agent. He tries to sell orders for this stuff from a catalogue he has. He wears something he calls a bush vest, with many pockets, and a hood in the collar and a pouch at the back. He calls it a 'walking desk'. It may have been suitable for Beirut, but it is wrong for Vanuatu. The polo thing and this selling around the pool make people very uneasy. He orders Gibsons from the pool bar, which is asking too much of the staff. Port Vila is not Acapulco.

He is very bad with the children.

He spoiled one little boy's holiday by asking him about his T-shirt. The T-shirt was quite nice and said 'Hullo from Gippsland Victoria'.

Evidently Blase asked the boy if he was from Gippsland.

When the boy said no, Blase asked him why he was wearing a T-shirt from Gippsland Victoria.

The boy had replied, 'My auntie sent it to me'.

Blase had then said to the boy that you wear a T-shirt either because you come from the place or because you've been to the place, and that you didn't wear a T-shirt because 'your auntie lives there'.

The boy then took the T-shirt off and was so badly sunburned that he was taken to hospital.

When the mother remonstrated with Blase about this, Blase said, 'What do you mean by making your son wear clothing his auntie sent him? No one wears clothes that aunties send'.

She then said, 'What about the clothes you wear about the pool? They aren't proper resort clothes'.

Blase then said to her, 'These clothes come from the Banana Republic Travel and Safari Clothing Company of Polk Street San Francisco'.

She replied that she didn't care whether the clothes came from Andres of Chifley Parade, Baulkham Hills, they weren't resort clothes, and in future to leave her little boy alone.

As Recreational Director I had to come between them.

And another thing – he has been trying to sell a Mosquito Repeller device which is supposed to give off ultra-sonic waves which duplicate the sound of an aggressive male mosquito. This supposedly scares away the female mosquito, which he says are the ones which sting.

Well, although one can't hear this thing, it is giving the staff and some of the guests ear-ache.

If he is your magazine's travel writer, he seems to be into all sorts of contra-deals and franchises which he is selling in your magazine's time around the pools and bars. He has about six watches on one arm, which he sells and which are a dubious bargain.

What I want to say is that this sort of person is bad for Vanuatu and bad for the travel industry. Why don't you send him back to Beirut, which needs a travel writer.

Signed, Recreation Director,
Inter-Continental Hotel, Port Vila, Vanuatu.

Hi Chief, It's true I'm in Vanuatu and it's true that Port Vila is not Acapulco. I'm resting up after cultural delegating in China.

The reaction against me here is because I joked about the plumbing. The plumbing in the Port Vila Inter-Continental is the loudest plumbing in the history of hotels. It should be mentioned as an attraction in their brochure. The velocity of the flush is so great that if you put your hand in the bowl it would be crushed. It can flatten a beer can. I kid you not. Every morning the hotel shakes to the thunder of 166 bowel movements and the roar of this flush is like the surf against the rocks. 'Flush' is too anaemic a verb to describe it. I hope it isn't all going into the azure lagoon out front.

Vanuatu is not really a holiday resort, it is a training resort for people getting ready to travel overseas. The airline is called Vanuatu Airlines and is painted to look like a coral reef, but it is really Ansett, and the hostesses are from Australia. There's no tipping, but people are trained to it because the government of Vanuatu takes 10 per cent of everything. Every bill is 10 per cent higher than the stated price.

Everywhere you go you see people learning to eat in restaurants, learning to sit around pools, learning to shop duty free, and learning to count in foreign money. But because Melanesia is so delightfully slow, they have time to learn how to do these things. They learn how to sign their signature exactly the way it is on the travellers cheque. They learn how to hold three official documents in one hand when coming through immigration control.

Frankly, I hang out at the Bar Rossi built in 1926, and I do my Somerset Maugham act on variety nights. My act is maybe a little too literary for the crowd, but I get a few laughs from the air hostesses to whom I have explained it.

I do a bit of dealing at the pool, but it is in my own time and anyhow no one's buying.

The two hardest things to do in Vanuatu are to get to eat the local speciality, flying fox, and to hear local music. It's so hard that I feel it is perhaps prohibited to tourists.

It is a good place for Australians to teach their children to be rude to people of a different colour and culture because the kids can get it right on the friendly Melanesians before they try it on American black waiters and Indian bell captains.

Of course, when I arrived I headed straight for the snorkeling deal to see the American Second-World-War wrecks. I wanted to see skeletons of American sailors trapped in the engine room and maybe bring up a rusty Smith and Wesson .45. All they showed me was a rusty anchor. And I got ear-ache.

People say that my Mosquito Repeller is giving then earache. It's the snorkeling.

As always at these sorts of resorts I spend most of the morning with the existential dilemma of whether to go for a swim or not. I never know whether to take money with me to the pool or whether to leave my watch in my room. If you take your wallet and watch and passport and you put them on the poolside table you get sore eyes from keeping them open under water watching your things. Everyone else seems to take their wallets to the pool. I get a wincing headache from the ripping of the Velcro fastenings of all those travel wallets. It is like a nurse ripping adhesive plaster from a body. I worry about putting on sunburn lotion properly, not missing any spot and reaching the middle of my back. Here in Vanuatu I smear it on the TV Screen and rub myself against it because they hit you 400 VTs a day for in-house movies and there's no television station and I'm not paying. I suppose the 400 VTs go to pay copyright to the people who made the films. Ho ho.

And what's the right time to hang out at the pool? When do the air hostesses go to the pool? And you have to decide whether to take a towel from your room which is against the rules. If you get a towel from the Recreation Director (which I do not for reasons I will not explain) you have to get it back by 6 p.m. But what happens if you want to get wet after 6 p.m.? What if the hostesses arrive after 6 p.m. and you want to do some fancy diving from the high board? Do you have your Gibson before the swim or after? I read of people dying from swimming after drinks. Does the wiping of the towel remove the sunburn lotion? What's the shower beside the pool for? Is it to wash off the chlorine after the swim or is it to wash your self before the swim? And who's saying who's dirty? If you had a shower before going to bed, and you didn't do anything dirty during the night, isn't that clean enough? Should you just splash about in the pool or should you do your seventy-five laps? How do you do laps in a kidney-shaped pool? People resent you lapping anyhow. They want to throw a ball to each other and when you plough through them they say things like,

'Jesus, here comes Mark Spitz again'. If the lotion comes off
when you swim, how can the pool be that clean anyhow? I tell
you one thing – don't talk to kids at the pool. I asked a kid about
his T-shirt and he took it off and got a touch of sun. All because
I said – I forget what I said. I hope his mother cuts herself on
coral and infection quickly sets in. If you've been sweating,
should you just dive into the pool? I see people doing that. I
point out to them that urine and sweat have the same chemical
constituents. So much for hygiene. Do kids pee in the water?
All the time. Is there a chemical which shows up whether the
kids are peeing in the pool? No. Do parents teach their kids not
to pee in the water? I doubt it. And would the kids take any
notice? No. If there are more than five kids in the pool I don't
go near it.

There is the lagoon but the Recreation Director gives orders
to the attendants to raise the sunbathing buoys so that I can't
get up on them. Petty. And I get runover by fun tigers and
wind-surfers and bumper boats.

I'm trying to get a polo team together to give the place a bit
of class. But there aren't any polo types here. I think I'll go up
to the Club Privé tonight. I told them I was the Night Club
writer and I get a good deal up there, but would you drop them
a note on letter-head paper? Thanks. I get 10 per cent at the
Forbidden Room too. It wouldn't hurt to drop them a note
also. I should perhaps go down to the Bar Rossi and catch the
sunset. Maybe there'll be a few new people in who haven't seen
the Somerset Maugham act. Maybe not. Decisions. Decisions. I
could maybe just pay the 400 VTs and get the keys to the
television set and just watch in-house movies. Then I'd have to
clean the gunk off the screen. Maybe I'll just crack the one-litre
bottle of Jack Daniel's and stay in my room (please leave all
mentions of brand names in. Wink, wink).
Cheers.

AMERICAN BAR

THE BARMAN WHO LOVED BOOKS

The barman who loved books worked in a New Orleans bar called Coeds. He told me he'd been to Mark Twain's house in Hartford, Connecticut and marvelled that Twain had built side chimneys on his open fireplace and put a window above the fireplace so that he could 'see the flames and watch the snowflakes falling at the same time.' The barman, named Joey, about 25, had a sort of barman-Twain wisdom which he would work-up and then come over from the cash register or the glass washer to present to me. The reason, he said, that he liked bus travel was that, 'you know you've travelled, I like to know that I've come some. Airplanes make you feel you've just gone next door except that you've got a headache. I like to know that I've made a journey.'

He'd met a student from Japan on a Greyhound bus when he'd been on his way to Hollywood to get into movies. Joey said this was before he'd discovered books. The Japanese student was on his way to Texas to 'see the cowboys'. To see the cowboys! Joey exclaimed, 'I thought how crazy can you get.'

But then later I saw myself. 'Here I am, going to Hollywood to get into movies,' so I thought: 'Which of us is crazy? We both had these crazy American ideas.'

HE ALSO LOVED PINBALL MACHINES

From time to time a patron of the bar would come over to Joey with a pinball problem. They would exchange stories of near ultimates and ornery balls. A student (it was a student bar) would get his two dollars worth of quarters and dat-dat-dat-dat-dat-dat-dat on the Balmy Bahama or the Shooting Sherrif 'motherfuckermotherfuckermotherfuckermotherfucker', lifting the corner of the machine and dropping it, bumping it with his hip, slapping it with his hand, 'motherfuckermotherfucker motherfucker'.

'Relax Harry,' Joey would call, 'time to relax.'

'Gimme two dollars quarters.'

I said, 'You're a real expert on the pinball machines Joey,' after hearing him give advice and tell his pinball stories.

He blushed, 'I spend a lot of time on the machines.'

But he wanted to talk about books.

'I don't want to write,' Joey said, 'I'm not ambitious, I just want to read, but gee, it's hard to get the time to read. You spend so much time getting to just eat.' With a fervour he talked of his reading hunger. 'And to think,' he said, 'I haven't even read all the Greats yet.' He stood leaning on the bar, both hands on the bar, shaking his head, 'I haven't read all Twain yet.'

'Jesus, so much to read. My chick and me, we heading for a crisis – she's in school, she gets home and she just wants to sit around watching teevee or reading comic books. And that's what she wants me to do.'

'Does she feel excluded if you read? Why does she object?'

'Yeah, I don't want to end up sitting around for the rest of my life watching teevee and eating teevee dinners.'

'Have you told her what you want?'

'Only a thousand times, she says she understands, but she has a way of forgetting, you know?'

He washed glasses, advised agitated pinball players to cool it, and sympathised with pinball players with near misses.

He cross-questioned me about what I did.

'Mr Blase, you shouldn't say that you're a writer,' he told me.

'Why not? That's how I try to earn a living.'

'It always sounds like you're out collecting material'. Which you are, but which you're not aware of at the time, or probing the human condition rather than, say, just getting drunk. Joey was right. But at least I'd burned my corduroy coat a year ago.

'It sets you apart,' Joey said, becoming Mark Twain.

'Now if Faulkner was to come in here,' Joey said, he wouldn't call himself a writer. He'd call himself a farmer.'

He went over to the cash register to think, and then came back.

'And you shouldn't be in here,' he gestured at the students in Coeds, 'you should get out and meet the people.'

'Who are the people?'

Joey smiled appreciatively, he knew that had a good, literary sound to it.

THE MAN WHO LOVED MOVIES

Joey introduced me to the man who loved movies.

'Now, meet Cliff here, where I like reading, Cliff he loves movies.'

'All I do,' said Cliff, 'is this: I study law; play poker; I go to the movies.'

He was about thirty. I have, by coincidence, the novel *The Movie Goer* by New Orleans writer, Walker Percy. I hold it up.

'Have you read it?' I said, more to Joey. 'No – gee I haven't read all the Greats yet.'

Cliff, the movie-goer, loved Lee Marvin. I said, 'Did you see *Point Blank*?'

'You've seen *Point Blank*!' He made an act of falling off his stool. 'We're the only two people in the world who've seen *Point Blank*. You've actually seen *Point Blank*?'

I said I'd seen it a number of times. (My mind flashing back to the Kogarah New Victory.)

'You saw it in Australia!'

'Yes.'

'Remember where Lee Marvin says to his buddy that you should never ask questions about a contract, and this time he breaks the rule and asks questions, and they both end up being shot?'

'Wasn't that *The Killers*?'

'Good God yes. Now let me get this straight. Let me tell you both stories so I can sort it out. You're right, that was *The Killers*.' Then he told the storylines of both movies, and where he reached a point of violence he would act it out with gestures and sound effects, graphically recreating it. Blam blam.

THE MAN WHO LOVED MOVIES ALSO LOVED VIOLENCE

Joey said to Cliff, 'You're really sick, you're sick about violence.'

'I like violence. I like grim realism,' Cliff said, matter-of-factly, not defensively. 'I took my nephews to see *The Cowboys*. I thought it was going to be strictly kids' matinee stuff, but I was pleasantly surprised.

'There was a lot of grim realism in it. A kid trampled to death by a herd of steer. Are you going to see it?' he asked me, stopping the story.

I said no, I didn't like Westerns with kids in them.

He went on, ' . . . the kids kill off the baddies one by one.
One baddy has his leg broken and his foot caught in the stirrup
and you know what the kids do? They don't free him. They
fire a shot into the air to set the horse running so that it drags
this guy along by his broken leg, his foot in the stirrup.'

Joey said, 'Now that's what I call really sick.'

'I like grim realism,' Cliff said, 'there wasn't any sex in it, but
it was a good film for grim realism.'

Joey said, 'I know all about violence. I was in the boxing
team at college. I never lost a fight. I go down the Quarter and
guys try to pick me. I won't fight. I'm not frightened, but I
don't want to be bothered anymore. It's not that I'm scared. I
don't have the time, it spoils the evening. I don't want to be
bothered.'

Cliff mentioned *Little Big Man* and said to Joey, 'Now if
you've got a feeling for the Indian situation you'd like it.'

'Cliff,' Joey said, 'I have a feeling for the Indian situation,
but the Indians don't get the dollar I pay to see *Little Big Man*. I
see myself as a patron of the arts,' he said, turning to me, 'if
someone lends me a book and I read it and I like it – I buy it. I
buy the hardback so that the writer gets something for his
work. If a writer has done a nice thing for me, I do something
for him. Take a book like Mark Twain's *Puddenhead Wilson* –
what a nice thing to have done for the world.'

JOEY'S MOVIE

'Before I discovered reading,' Joey said, ' – and I didn't discover
reading at college – I wanted to go into films. I got this stake
together and decided I'd go to Hollywood and get into movies.
I bought a Greyhound bus ticket and we go across Texas and we
get to the Pecos. Now everything's supposed to happen West
of the Pecos. That's supposed to be the turning point. West of
the Pecos. Well there are ten guys on the bus all stretched out

on the seats. Everyone is in a bad mood. We're probably all going to Hollywood to get into the movies. They don't even make them there any more. But what happens at the Pecos. A luscious broad gets in. Really magnificent and she gets in right at Pecos – right on midnight. Where does she sit?

'She sits right opposite me. She takes out a cigarette. I out with my matches, working up a quick line about, 'where are you going' and so on. I lean across to light her cigarette and before I can speak she says, "Come and sit by me." She asked me! Next thing she pulls out this marihuana and we smoke and she gets really friendly to me and we end up doing everything you can on a Greyhound bus which is everything. It was as if everything was happening West of the Pecos; it was everything I wanted. Everything I dreamed about. Like a movie. We get to El Paso, and she says well, this is where I get off, lover, this is where we part. I said, "But this can't be – no way – this can't be." She agreed to have breakfast with me.

'I bought it with change, all I had, out of the machines at the Greyhound station. I kept saying, "This can't be – you can't just go." But she says, "This is the way it's got to be" and just goes off. The most beautiful woman I've ever seen.'

'There was sex in *The Cowboys*,' Cliff said, 'I remember now. There was a wagon load of whores.' He gives us the dialogue and re-enacts the scene for us, completely ignoring Joey's story. 'They agree, see, that the first time for a boy should be in the back of a wagon with a girl he thinks he loves.'

'Or in the back of a Greyhound bus,' I said irresistibly.

COED'S BAR

Coed's has four pinball machines, trays of coloured lights and electrified movement in a dark bar.

The barman has to give customers a torch so that they can see to write cheques. It is an undergraduate bar. No one can see

your acne in Coed's Bar. There are T-shirts for sale, with
'Coed's Bar' stencilled on them. An ornamental football with
'Tulane' on it. A poster saying 'Let's get together'. Juke box,
tables and chairs, and stools at the bar.

THE AIR-CONDITIONING MAN

It wasn't his bar any more than it was mine. He was in air-conditioning from New York. He was a conservative and a bigot.
He liked Australia because we had a small population and no
blacks. He thought about moving to Australia after he retired.
He thought that Australia was an anti-welfare state. I told him,
not really. He bemoaned the state of the American nation. I told
him that it had to do with air-conditioning.
    I said that air-conditioning had made the people soft.
    I said that there wasn't much air-conditioning in Australia.
We were a tougher nation. Survivors. I said I grew up without
glass in the windows, let alone air-conditioning.
    He became unsettled. 'By god, you know I think you're onto
something.' He decided that air-conditioning, in which he'd
worked for a lifetime, could seriously have contributed to the
weakening of the morale and fibre of the United States. He was
seriously unsettled.
    I left him, to have some Dandy Fried Chicken, and clams.

PART TWO

ORAL HISTORY OF A CHILDHOOD

Mechanical Aptitude

Pass the Stillsons. They are not the Stillsons. I told you what the Stillsons were last time. These are the Stillsons. Now stand out of the way. Do you always have to stand in the light. No, that's not the one. I wanted the small one. Do I have to do everything myself? Now you're spilling it everywhere. Well, be more careful in future. In future use your head. Just take it slowly, you're spilling it, you're spilling it on my boots. Wake up Australia. your mind's a thousand miles away. You've put that on the wrong way around. It's screwed on back to front. How did you manage to do that? You can't find it. How can you not find it? If it were a snake it would bite you. How do you mean 'it just came off'? How could it 'just come off'? Why do these things happen to you and to no one else? Now stand out of the light. Now look what you've done. Your wouldn't know it from a bar of soap. You wouldn't know if it was up you. If it was any nearer it would bite you. Look where you're going, for godsake. Two left feet. Not that way, do it the way I showed you. All thumbs. How did it take so long? Where the hell did you get to? The lavatory – how many times a day do

you have to go to the lavatory.? Now pass that piece up to me.
Not that piece – the other piece. How many times do I have to
tell you? You don't listen. Here, give it to me, I'll do it myself.
Not that way, the other way. It's self explanatory. Well, no one
asked your opinion. Well, it's not up to you. What, precisely,
do you think you're doing now? Well your best isn't good
enough. Watch out behind you. Watch out you'll break that
window. Take that smirk off your face – it's no laughing
matter. I wouldn't want to have my life depending on it. I
wouldn't want to be holding my breath. So's Christmas. Don't
waste it. It's not hot enough. You've let it go cold. How did
that get chipped? Look at that mess. You call that tidy! What
about in the corners? Don't force it. Hey dreamy, wake up –
Australia needs you. You wouldn't know if it was up you. I'll
explain it all once more, I'm not going to tell you again. Look
where you're going for Christsake. Is that what you call sharp?
Can't you tell just by looking at it. Where do you think you're
going now? Looking isn't going to fix it. What time do you
think it is? It screws out, it doesn't pull out. Watch out for that
wall. Come here and watch so that you'll know next time.
Don't stand in the light. Just stay out of the road. What do you
think this is – a picnic? What do you think this is – bush week?
Well, there may not be a next time. Now look what you've
done. It's no laughing matter. How long's a piece of string. If
brains were dynamite you'd be safe. Where were you when the
brains were handed out. Take the other end. This end, not that
end. Not that way. Now get a proper grip of it. You're holding
it like a girl. You take as long as an old woman. Left to right,
not right to left. Clockwise, not anti-clockwise. No, the other
way, dummy. Measure it again. Use a little elbow grease. Use a
little nous. Use a little brain power. Use a little brawn. Fellows
of Australia, blokes and coves and coots, get a bloody move on,
have some bloody sense. Measure it before you cut it. Hold it
straight. It's as crooked as a dog's hind leg. That's not how I

showed you. Now do it again, and get it right this time. That's
not very smart. Don't they teach you anything at school. And
you're supposed to be bright. Now look what you've gone and
done? Start over again. Holy cow – how did you manage to do
that? It's in the bottom compartment of the tool box at the back
of the truck under the coils of wire, the black-handled one, not
the other one, and the tinsnips and a five-eights coach-head
screw. What do you mean, you can't see it? Use your eyes. I
told you to check it before you did it. And put things back
where you found them. What sort of knot do you call that?
That nut doesn't go with that bolt. Can't you just tell. That's
not mixed enough. That's not hard enough. That's not long
enough. It won't bite you. Take hold of it. It's not going to eat
you. Easy does it. You're worse than a girl. Get a move on, we
haven't got all day. Shine the torch where I'm working. No not
there, over here. Hold it steady. Now pull. Pull harder. That's
enough, for godsake. Now look what you've gone and done. In
future, stop when I say stop. Don't jerk it. You'll strip the
thread. Can't you get it tighter than that? Now I'll tell you
once more: this is the nosing, this is the waist, and this is the
riser, and this is the thread, and this is called the going, and this
is called the going of the flight, and we call this the raking rise.
Got it? Frightened to get your hands dirty? Frightened of a few
blisters? Short of puff? Put your hand in and get it out. It won't
bite you . Don't just stand there, do something. What are you –
an old woman? No one asked your opinion. Get your finger
out. Get a move on. What did I tell you? What do you mean
you can't see it? What do you mean you can't find it? What do
you mean you didn't bring it? What do you mean you left it
behind? What do you mean you thought we wouldn't need it?
What do you mean you didn't think it mattered. Watch out for
the wall, for godsake. Do it once and do it right. You can't
possibly see from over there. Don't throw it, hand it to me. Do
I have to do everything myself? Now look what you've gone

and done. Frightened to get your hands dirty. It won't eat you. You're worse than a girl. What do you mean, you didn't think it mattered? And what, precisely, do you think you're doing now?

PLEDGES, VOWS AND PASS THIS NOTE

Pass this note. He wants an answer. Pass this note on and do not read it. He wants an answer. Will you be my girlfriend? I like you: do you like me? Meet me after school, but do not tell anyone. Do you like being tickled? Do you like being held down? Do you like being chased and caught? Do you like hiding and being found? Do you like being blindfolded and turned around and around? Do you like being tied up? Father Uncle Cousin Kin. FM ʟ JL true. What's your name? Would you like a hot milkshake? Don't use a straw. We'll all meet at the pictures and swap seats. I'll walk you home. Yes, but I have to be home by eleven. Do you know what tickling the palm means? Have you ever been kissed with your mouth open? FM ʟ MC true. What's your name? Can I take you to the school dance? Do I have to come in and meet your parents? Would you like coffee and raisin toast? May I walk you home? Yes, but I have to be home by twelve. Have you ever tongue-kissed before? I've never kissed a girl like this before. I bet you say that to all the girls. FM ʟ NJ true. FM ʟ JS true. FM ʟ FL true. FM ʟ JJ true. I love you and I'll love you until the twelfth of never

and that's a long, long time. Dearest. My dearest. My darling.
Darling. Yours forever. Only yours. SWALK. With all the
love in my heart. They tried to tell us we're too young, too
young to really be in love.
Please don't do that.
Not there. Not yet.
I'm not that sort of girl.
I promised my mother I wouldn't.
I want to do it, but I don't think now is the right time.
Marke but this flea, and marke in this,
How little that which thou deny'st me is;
Mee it suck'd first, and now sucks thee,
And in this flea, our two bloods mingled bee . . .
Be patient with me.
When I'm surer of my feelings.
But I do love you.
When it's safe.
I want the first time to be beautiful.
Had we but World enough, and Time,
This coyness Lady were no crime . . .
But at my back I alwaies hear
Time's winged Chariot hurrying near.
But we have our whole life ahead of us.
I don't want to feel guilty about it.
I don't want it to be furtive.
I don't want it to be something we just do.
But I do love you.
How little that which thou deny'st me is . . .
Love oh love oh careless love.
I'm very nervous.
Be gentle.
You must never tell anyone.
Have you ever done it with anyone else?
Was that nice for you?

We are man and wife now, even if the world doesn't know it.
Going out together. Going around together. Going steady.
Sort of engaged. On together.
That's all you think of now when we go out.
One-track mind.
Don't you ever think of anything else?
No, I want to see the end of the movie.
Men are all the same.
You only like me because I let you do it.
But I saw you with her in the coffee shop.
How could you?
I'm not jealous.
I just don't like two-timers.
You're free to do what you want and I'm free to do what I
    want.
I think it will give us time to see if we really love each other.
We'll call it off then.
We've broken up. We've busted up. He broke it off.
It's all over between us.
I missed you too.
The best part of breaking up is making up.
This time is for keeps.
But don't ever do that to me again, promise?
Don't you ever think of anything else?
You only like me because I let you do it.
But I saw you looking at her.
Really, I'm different.
We'll call it off then.
We've broken up. We've busted up. I broke it off.
I've given him up as a bad job.
It's all over between us.
What's your name? Would you like to go for a drive?
Not on the first date.
We hardly know each other.

How little that which thou deny'st me is ...
Let's get to know each other a little better.
Had we but World enough, and Time,
This coyness Lady were no crime ...
If you really love someone it's OK.
I love you and I'll love you until the twelfth of never and
    that's a long long time.
Love oh love oh careless love.
FM L WH true.
We were made for each other.
But what if we had a baby?
True love has a guardian angel on high with nothing to do,
    but to care for you and to care for me, love forever true.
    But that's all you want to do now when we go out.
It was different at first.
One-track mind.
Don't you ever think of anything else?
There's something you should know.
I can't tell you over the telephone.
I'm overdue.
Sorry, false alarm.
I'm afraid I have something pretty important to tell you.
Of course I'm sure.
This time I'm sure.
You're going to be a father.
How does that grab you?
I'm pregnant. I'm with child. I'm expecting, I'm in the
    pudding club. I'm in the family way. Bun in the oven.
Of course it's yours ... I resent that.
No ... I won't find out the name of a doctor.
The cold light of day.
If we love each other everything will be alright.
I want a proper wedding.
Well you'll have to tell them sooner or later.

I'll only say love and honour I won't say obey.
Dearly beloved we are gathered together here in the sight of
    God, and in the face of this congregation, to join together
    this Man and this Woman in holy Matrimony.
My very dearest wife.
My very dearest husband.
Will you still find me attractive after I've had children?
Will you still love me when my looks are gone?
Will you still love me when I'm old and grey?
Will you still love me when you have to look across at me
    every morning at the breakfast table?
A penny for them.
What goes on in your head?
Talk to me just once in a while.
It may have escaped your notice, but I live here too.
You'd feel better if you talked about it.
It says in the magazines that it is better to talk.
You keep everything inside you.
But how could you : She's my best friend!
But how could you : She's old enough to be your mother!
But how could you : She's been with everyone in town!
So it's come to this has it?
There's a race of men that don't fit in,
It's a race that can't be still,
So they break the hearts of kith and kin,
And they roam the world at will.
Poetry doesn't mend anything.
I can forgive you but it will never be the same again.
Don't touch me.
If you won't talk to me will you talk to a doctor?
It's a race that can't be still,
    so they break the hearts of kith and kin, and they roam the
world at will.
Alright then, that's it, is it?

Alright then, is that all you have to say?
Alright then, it's come to this has it?
Alright then, you can tell your mother and father, I'm not.
Alright then, but don't expect baby and me to be here when
   you come crawling back.
And they roam the world at will.

PLAYGROUND JUSTICE AND BEING FAIR

Heads I win, tails you lose. Granny's rules. Last in's lousy. I'll fight you for it. It's my turn now. Fair's fair. You had first go last time. But you can be first next time. You said that yesterday. You can be first tomorrow. But tomorrow never comes. No playing favourites. But that's not fair. Granny's rules. That's cheating. Come on, fair go. Cheats don't prosper. Flukes don't count. Who says it's a fluke. Granny's rules. Best out of three. Who says. I say. How do you get to say. Because I'm the oldest and you're the youngest. I bags it. But I saw it first. Finderskeepers Losersweepers. Who says. I say. Because I'm the biggest. Swap you. I'll lend it to you until lunchtime. But you've go two. Share and share alike. Fair's fair. Fair share. Share and and share alike. Fair's fair. Fair share. Go you halves. Don't be a crybaby. Don't be a cissy. Don't be yellow. Take it like a man. Learn to take your medicine. But you hit below the belt. Don't be a bad sport. You lost your temper. Because I'm bigger than you. Because if you don't I'll tell my brother. Pick on someone your own age. Pick on someone your own size. But you ganged up on me. You'll cop it. You'll get yours. I'll get you back for that. I'll get my own back, you'll see. You promised not to tell. You dobbed me in. Now we're quits. You're on my side. I'll stick up for you if you'll stick up for me. I won't tell on you if you don't tell on me. You're not in this game. Because we say you're not. Coming ready or not. First to the tree and back gets it. Because they're the rules. Who says. I say. Why. Because I'm the biggest. Granny's rules. Bet you I'm right. Shake on it. I'm the boss of the game. Why. Because I own the bat. That doesn't count, I'll give you a start. Bags be first. Because I had my fingers crossed. Fair's fair. Do us a favour. Tell tale tittle tongue your tongue will split and the puppy dogs will all get a bit. Let's vote on it. Because you're a girl. Because girls don't count. Because you're too little. They're all your friends. Promise not to tell. You'll be sorry. I'll be in it if you'll be in it. I won't tell on you if you don't tell on me. I'm the King of the Castle and you're the dirty rascal. Silence in the court the monkey wants to talk the first one to talk is a monkey. Wait for me you promised. But you promised. Cross your heart and spit your death. On your honour. On your oath. I'll fight you for it. Let's go halves. Fair's fair. Share and share alike. Shake on it.

I tortured Jenny Little, now an actress in London, with the Chinese burn. Telephone Jenny Little in East Sheen and ask her if she remembers being tortured at Nowra Infants School near the Headmistress's garden with the Chinese burn. The garden where you found nuts you could shoot at each other's eyes with your thumb. Along from the trees which at the right time of the year provided the rough nuts on the end of a stalk, a blow from which could cause a headache. Or if these were out of season, you could roll your handkerchief and twist it into a cosh which each year had to be banned because of headaches. You had to be careful or the girls would hold you down and kiss you. Finger cracking will make your knuckles larger. Being double-jointed was a good thing and could be demonstrated now and then when remembered. Blushing, warts, ear wax, toe jam, snot eating, and excreta smells were something to watch for in others and to be quickly pointed out with derision until the person cried. Farts should always be denied. Muscle biceps were to be developed by flexing and lifting of weights when remembered. If you wanted to be a commando. Chinese burns were inflicted by grasping the flesh of the forearm with both

hands and twisting one hand clockwise and the other other-
wise. Tongue poking was always an insult and deserved retalia-
tion. Face pulling could be used to force someone to laugh and
get them into trouble, but you had to watch for the wind
changing. Holding up your little finger would always make
someone laugh, if you kept a straight face. Tortures apart from
the dreaded Chinese burn, included forcing someone to the
ground, sitting on them, pinning their arms with your knees
and drumming on their chests with your fingers, or the
Chinese water torture – dripping water on their forehead drop
by drop until they went mad and were never the same again,
which we never got right, or by bringing the blade of a pocket
knife close to the throat, or by tickling the feet or armpits or by
holding someone's nose and covering their mouth until they
smothered. Or gagging someone with a dirty handkerchief and
tying them up and leaving them. Tortures can be use to extract
secrets or to make someone cry. You can give yourself a 240-
volt shock by biting hard on both little fingers, linking the
fingers and pulling sharply. If the light shines through the
palms of you hand when you hold a torch to it you will always
be broke when you grow up. If the letter M appears in the lines
on the palms of your hands you'll marry. A blow to the temple
will kill, a blow to the throat will cause choking (ask Clive
Robertson, who was hit near the bubblers). You can hit
someone in the throat if he is older. A blow to stomach will
cause winding, a blow to the jaw will cause unconsciousness.
No hitting below the belt. No punching in the kidneys. Is
being unconscious the same as being asleep or is it more like
being hypnotised? What's being hypnotised like? What happens when a girl faints like Isabella Smart. Place your palms
together, cross your thumbs: if the left thumb goes over the
right you're artistic. The monkey grip cannot be broken. You'll
die if you swallow your tongue. If you have flat feet you cannot
join the commandos and you'll never win a race. If you close
your eyes and hold your breath, black will become white and

you will see the stars. Holding your breath underwater until you see stars is good for your condition. If you punch with your thumb inside your fist you'll break your thumb. Girls can spit, bite, slap, pinch and pull hair. Boys can punch, thump, strangle and kick. Turning around in circles with your eyes shut is a way of making yourself sick if you have to. If you rub hair oil in your hands or pepper tree leaves, a caning won't hurt. Never admit to an enemy that anything can hurt you. Can you whistle by putting your little fingers in the corners of your mouth? A boy may pinch a girl's backside, but nowhere else, A girl can pinch anywhere. Boys can tickle girls, and vice versa. Tickling someone can send them mad. You blind a cat by putting soap powder in its eyes which could be used against an enemy, or pepper. You can give someone a horse bite by savagely grasping the flesh at the top of the arm with your hand. You can give someone a rabbit killer by chopping them on the back of the neck with the edge of hand. You can give a cork leg by kicking someone's thigh with your knee. Can you pat your head and rub your stomach at the same time? Can you touch your nose with your tongue? Can you roll your eyes until only the whites are showing? If you hold someone's arm in a bucket of water they'll have to go to the lavatory. If you make the other person's nose bleed you've won. If you pin someone's arm to the ground to the count of three, you've won. If you twist someone's arm up their back until they say give in, you've won. Eating raw ginger and standing on your head for long periods are ways of becoming tough. You can stick a pin through the skin of your finger and it doesn't hurt. If you suck the soft part of your under arm you can give yourself a love bite. Knuckles is the toughest game there is. Hold your clenched fist against another boy's fist and count one-two-three. The fastest boy brings his knuckles down on the other's knuckles as hard as he can, causing immense pain. Drinking ink can kill you. Filling your mouth with water and wiping away any trace of it and then going up to someone and spitting it in their face is a form of surprise attack. Wiping snot on someone is another form of attack. Squeezing someone just above the knee with two fingers is a way of testing if they're jealous. If hairs grow on your legs it means you're becoming a man. If you hate hairs on your legs you shouldn't admit it. If you close your eyes while cleaning your teeth you're a homosexual. Hairs on the palms of your hands means you masturbate. If you look to see – that proves it. Grabbing another boy's cock is supposed to hurt and he is supposed to do it back to you. You're not supposed to show you like it. Wrestling until you get an erection is permissible as long as you both pretend it's a wrestle. A possum bite comes back at the same time every year at the same place you were bitten. A hanging willow makes good whips for whipping slave girls. When the girl who is playing nurse bandages your legs with dock leaves and binds them with vines, things happen in your groin. Girls walk differently after they've had their first sex. And you can tell.

Part Three

Death: Remedies: Convalescence

THE DROVER'S WIFE

Memo Editor:
Chief, I picked this paper up while hanging out at the Conference on Commonwealth Writing in Milan. This Italian student, Franco Casamaggiore, seems to be onto something. As far as I know it's a scoop, me being the only press around. I'd go with it as the cover story if I were you. This study of Australian culture is a big deal here in Europe – twenty six universities have courses on Australian writing. I'm hanging out angling for a professorship or something like that. This Casamaggiore has got a few of his facts wrong, but the subs can pick those up. Great stuff, eh! He could do for the Merino what Blainey did for Asians. (The inspired Suzanne Kiernan helped me with the translation.)

CONFERENCE PAPER BY FRANCO CASAMAGGIORE

The writing of a story called *The Drover's Wife* by Henry Lawson in 1893, the painting of a picture called *The Drover's Wife* by Russell Drysdale in 1945, and the writing of another

story by the same name in 1975, by Murray Bail, draws our
attention to what I will argue in this paper, is an elaborate
example of a national culture joke, an 'insider joke' for those
who live in that country – in this example, the country of
Australia. Each of these works has the status of an Australian
classic and each of these works, I will show, contains a joking
wink in the direction of the Australian people which they
understand but which non-Australians do not. The joke draws
on the colloquial Australian humour surrounding the idea of a
drover's 'wife'.

First, a few notations of background for those who are
unfamiliar with Australian folklore and the occupation of a
drover, which is corruption of the word 'driver'. The drover or
driver of sheep literally drove the sheep to market. The sheep,
because of health regulations governing strictly the towns and
cities of Australia, were kept many kilometres inland from the
sea-market towns. The sheep had then to be 'driven' by the
driver or drover from inland to the towns, often many thousands of kilometres, taking many months. I am told that this
practice has ceased and the sheep are now housed in the cities in
high-rise pens.

The method of driving the sheep was that each sheep
individually was placed in a wicker basket on the backs of
bullock-drawn wagons known as the woollen wagons. This
preserved the sheep in good condition for the market. These
bullocks, it is said, could pull the sheep to the coast without
human guidance, if needed, being able, of course, to smell the
sea. But the sheep had to be fed and the drover or driver would
give water and seed to the sheep during the journey. The wagon
in the Drysdale painting is horse-drawn, denoting a poorer
peasant-class of drover. The wagon in the painting would
probably hold a thousand sheep in wicker baskets.

Now the length of the journey and the harshness of condi-
tions precluded the presence of women and the historical fact is
that for a century or more there were no women in this

pioneering country. This, understandably, led men to seek
other solace in this strange new country. Australian historians
acknowledge the closeness of men under this condition of
pioneering and have described it as mateship, or a pledging of
unspoken alliance between two men, a marriage with vows
unspoken.

Quite naturally too, with the drover or driver, a close and
special relationship grew between him and his charges who
became an object for emotional and physical drives, but this
remains unacknowledged by historians for reasons of national
shame, but is widely acknowledged by the folk culture of
Australia. And now acknowledged by art. Interspecies reciprocity. Hence the joke implicit in the use by two writers and a
painter of the title *The Drover's Wife* and the entry of this
unacceptable historical truth from the oral culture to high
culture via coded humour and until this paper (which I
modestly consider a breakthrough study) absent from academic
purview.

I elicited the first inklings of this from answers received to
questions asked of Australian visitors to Italia about the sheep
droving. First, I should explain. Unfortunately, I am a poor
student living in a humble two-room tugurio. It is a necessity
for me to work in the bar of the Hotel Principe e Savoia in
Milano and for a time before that, in the Gritti Palace Hotel
Venezia. If the authorities would provide more funds for
education in this country maybe Italia would regain its rightful
place at the forefront of world culture. But I wander from my
point. This experience in the bar work gave me the opportunity
on many occasions to talk and question visiting Australians,
although almost always men.

There is an Australian humour of the coarse peasant type not
unknown in Italia. Without becoming involved in these details
it is necessary for me to document some of the information
harvested from contact with the Australian, not having been to
the country at first hand – thanks to the insufficiency of funds

from the educational authorities in Italia – however, my brother Giovanni is living there in Adelaide, but is not any help in such matters, knowing nothing of the droving or culture and knowing only of the price of things and the Holden automobile. Knowing nothing of things of the spirit. You are wrong, Giovanni.

Yes, but to continue. A rubber shoe or boot used when hunting in wet weather called the gun boot was used by the drovers or drivers and found to be a natural love aid while at the same time a symbol used in a gesture of voluntary submission by the drover before his charge.

The boots were placed on the hind legs of the favoured sheep. The drover would be shoeless like the sheep and the sheep would 'wear the boots' (cf. 'wearing pants' in marriage). The toe of the boots would be turned towards the drover who would stand on the toes of the boot thus holding the loved sheep close to him in embrace. These details suffice.

According to my Australian informants the sheep often formed an emotional attachment to the drover who reciprocated. But the journey to the coast had its inherent romantic tragedy. The long journey and shared hardship, shared shelter, the kilometres of companionship, daily took them closer to the tragic conclusion with the inevitable death of the loved one through the workings of capitalist market forces. But also the return of the drover's natural drives to his own species as he re-entered the world of people. And the limited vision of the anti-life Church.

'Why not dogs?' comes the question. Close questioning of my Australian sources suggests that dogs as bed companions was characteristic of the Aboriginal and thus for reasons of racial prejudice considered beneath the Australian white man. The sheep from Europe was a link with the homelands from whence he had migrated and further, I speculate, that the maternal bulk of the merino sheep, with its woolly coat and large soft eyes, its comforting bleat, offered more feminine solace than the lean dog with fleas. Again, on this and other matters, Giovanni is of no assistance being concerned only with his Holden automobile and the soccer football. The unimaginative reaction of the educational authorities for research funding for this project indicts our whole system of education in this country.

Returning now to the art works under study. In Henry Lawson's story the woman character lives out her life *as if she were a sheep.* She is not given a name – in English animal husbandry it is customary to give cows names (from botany) and domestic pets are named, but not sheep. The scholar Keith Thomas says that a shepherd however, could recognise his sheep by their faces. She is penned up in her outback fold, unable to go anywhere. Her routines of the day resemble closely the life of a sheep and it can be taken that this is a literary transformation for the sake of propriety. She tells in the story how she was taken to the city a few times in a 'compartment', as is the sheep. In the absence of her drover husband she is looked after by a dog, as is a sheep. The climax of the Henry Lawson story is the 'killing of the snake' which needs no Doctor Freud, being the expression of a savage and guilt-ridden male detumescence (in Australia the male genitalia is referred to in folklore, as the 'one-eyed trouser snake'. The Australian folk language is much richer than its European counterpart, which is in state of decay). I am told that to this day, Australian men are forever killing the snake. The drover is absent from the story, a point to be taken up later.

In the Drysdale painting (1945) oddly and fascinatingly, there are no sheep. Then we realise uneasily that it is as if they have been swept up into a single image overwhelming the foreground – the second drover's 'wife'. This unusually shaped woman is, on second glance, in the form of a sheep, a merino sheep, the painter having given her the same maternal physical bulk as the merino. Her shadow forms the shape of a sheep. Again, the drover is all but absent. He is a background smudge.

The snake, you ask? In the trees we find the serpents. They writhe before our eyes.

Murray Bail is a modern Australian long removed from the days of pioneering and droving. However, his biography reveals that his father was a drover, but our discipline requires us to disregard this fact when considering his work of art. In his contemporary story he pays homage both to the Drysdale painting and the Lawson story. In the Bail story the woman is referred to as having one defining characteristic, what author Bail calls a 'silly streak'. This is a characteristic traditionally ascribed to sheep (cf. 'woolly minded'). The woman figure in this Bail story, or precisely the 'sheep figure', wanders in a motiveless way; strays, as it were; away from the city and her dentist husband. Curious it is to note that she flees the man whose work it is to care for the teeth which are the instrument used to eat the sheep, and for the sheep, symbol of death. Recall: the journey from the inland paradise in the protection of a loving drover to the destination of death: the city and the slaughterhouse and finally the teeth of the hungry city. In the Bail story the woman goes from the arms of her natural predator, the one who cares for the predator's teeth – the dentist – into the arms of the natural protector, the drover or driver. The Bail story reverses the tragedy and turns it to romantic comedy. Again, the drover himself is absent from the story. The Bail story also has a 'killing of the snake'.

So, in all three works of High Art under discussion we have three women clearly substituting (for reasons of propriety) for sheep, but coded in such a way as to lead us, through the term 'drover's wife' back into the folk culture and its joke. And we note that in the three works there is *no drover*. This is a reversal of situation, an inside-out-truth, for we know historically that *there was a drover* but there was historically *no wife*, not in any acceptable conventional sense.

The question comes, given that the drover has a thousand sheep in his care, how did the drover choose, from that thousand, just one mate? This question, intriguing and bizarre at the same time, was put to my Australian sources. Repeatedly I also ask Giovanni to ask the other men at GMH factory, but he has a head that is too full of materialism to concern himself with exploration of the mythology of this new culture.

How was the sheep chosen? But as in all matters of the human emotion the answer comes blindingly plain. It was explained to me that it is very much like being in a crowded lift, or in a prison, or on board a ship. In a situation of confinement it is instinctive for people to single out one another from the herd. There is communication by eye, an eye-mating, the search for firstly, mate, and then community. The same it is with sheep, my Australian sources tell me (thanks to educational authorities of Italia I have no chance to research this first hand). In the absence of human contact the eyes wander across species, the eyes meet, the eyes and ewes (that is English language pun).

Yes, and the question comes, was I being fooled about by these Australian visitors and their peasant humour after they had drunk perhaps too much? Was I being 'taken in' as they, the Australians say. I ask in return – were the Australian visitors telling more than they knew or wanted to tell? The joking is a form of truth telling, a way of confession. They were also by joking with my questions, trying to make me look away from my enquiry. To joke away something that was too painfully serious. But they were also telling me what they did not wish me to know as outsider, for the confession is precisely this, and brings relief. They experience an undefined relief from their joking about such matters – that is, the relief of confession. I let them joke at me for it was the joke to which I listened not them. This is the manoeuvre of the national joke, the telling and the not telling at the same time. So yes, I was being 'taken in' by my Australian sources – 'taken in' to the secret. Taken in to their confidence.

We are told that humour has within it the three dialogues.

The dialogue between the teller and the listener, where the teller is seeking approval and giving a gift at the same time. The dialogue between the teller's unconscious mind and his voice, to which the teller cannot always listen. The dialogue between the joker, teller, and the racial memory which is embodied in the language and the type of joke the teller chooses to tell, the well of humour from which the joker must draw his bucket of laughter. Humour is the underground route that taboo material – or material of national shame – must travel, and it is the costume it must wear.

Today such relations between sheep and men are, of course, rare in Australia. However, the racial memory of those stranger and more primitive days – days closer, can we say, to nature and a state of grace – still lingers. It is present in a number of ways. As illustrated, it is present in the elaborate cultural joke of High Art. The art which winks. It is there in the peasant humour of the male Australian, the joke which confesses. It is present, I would argue (here I work from photographs and cinema), in the weekly ritual called 'mowing the lawn'. On one afternoon of the weekend the Australian male takes off grass from his suburban garden which in earlier times would have been fodder for the sheep – this is an urban 'hay-making ritual', Australian city man's last connection with agriculture. But, alas, his sheep is gone, and the grass, the hay, is burned, to a memory of an association all but forgotten. Finally, I am told that there is an Australian national artefact – the sheepskin with wool attached. It is used often as a seat cover in the automobile. That today the driver or drover of a car sits (or lies) with sheep, as it were, under him while driving not a flock of sheep but a family in a modern auto. It gives comfort through racial memory far exceeding the need for warmth in that temperate land. The car sheepskin covering is an emotional trophy from the sexual underworld of the Australian past. The artefact which remembers.

Naturally, all this is still not an open subject for academic explicitness in Australia and it is only here in Italia where such candour can be enjoyed with our perspective of centuries – and our knowledge of such things. But I say, Australia – be not ashamed of that which is bizarre, seek not always the genteel. Remember that we, the older cultures, have myths which also acknowledge such happenings of interspecies reciprocity (cf. Jason and Search for Golden Fleece). See in these happenings the beginnings of you own mythology. See it as an affirmation of the beautiful truth – that we share the plant with animals and we are partners, therefore in its destiny.

So, in Lawson, Drysdale and Bail, we see how High Art in this new culture, admits a message of unspeakable truth (albeit, in a coded and guilty way), this being the ploy of all great national cultures.

Thus is the magic of the imagination.

LETTER TO THE GENERAL MANAGER OF THE ABC

Post Office
Coolangatta

To The General Manager
ABC
Sydney

Dear Sir,
I wish to enlighten you as to what is going on over the air, as I am certain you will not stand for it.

On Wednesday night I switched on to radio station 2NR a programme, I think, coming from Sydney, portraying among other things Henry Lawson's 'The Drover's Wife' and Russell Drysdale's painting 'The Drover's Wife'.

The Narrator was introduced as Professor someone and was stated to be an Italian who himself claimed to have worked in bars. This is how it went.

According to this Italian early Australian Drovers were so short of women that they had affairs with sheep . . .

. . . I switched off then – I couldn't stand any more I am so annoyed now 2 days later that I have a job to write.

I am an old drover of sheep and cattle and many of my friends are. I am married with children and grandchildren. These people need kicking out. I've never heard anything so vile and distasteful.

They should never be allowed near a broadcasting microphone to misrepresent decent men and women of Australia.

Sincerely (name withheld).

LETTER TO THE BULLETIN

THAT'S WHAT YOU SAY

The Drover's Wife
I refer to the article which appeared in the Centenary Edition of the *Bulletin*, page 160. The article in question is a transcription of a paper on Australian culture given 'excitedly' by an Italian student, one Franco Casamaggiore, at a recent conference on Commonwealth writing in Milan.

Without wishing to pour cold water on any excited students, I do however, wish to draw attention to some obvious fallacies regarding the interpretation of Henry Lawson's story 'The Drover's Wife' presented in this article and therefore at the conference in Milan. Incidentally Mr Lawson's story also appears in this edition of the *Bulletin*, page 257.

Firstly, it is claimed that the woman character lives her life 'as if she were a sheep. She is penned up in her outback fold, unable to go anywhere. Her routines of the day resemble closely the

life of a sheep and it can be taken that this is a literary
transformation for the sake of propriety. She tells in the story
how she was taken to the city a few times in a compartment, as
is the sheep. She is looked after by a dog, as is the sheep.'

This is an over-simplification. She is not penned up. She has
no buggy, but she has a horse and if she wanted to leave she
could. She stays because she is loyal, not because of any fences.
Every Sunday she and the children dress up and go for a ritual
stroll along the bush track. The bush is vast and sometimes it
depresses her, but she is not penned up by it. And how do her
daily routines resemble those of a sheep? I have never yet seen a
sheep preparing and cooking food; washing or mending
clothes or sweeping the floor, let alone reading the *Young Ladies
Journal*. Furthermore I think it highly unlikely that the sleeping compartment of the railway carriage which her husband
hired for her trip to the city could be compared to a sheep pen
on the same railway even though the occasional grumblings of
railway travellers of the day might do so. She and the dog are
companions – surely the dog can be a woman's friend as well as
a man's. Very different from the working sheepdog.

The article continues . . . 'The climax of the Henry Lawson
story is the "killing of the snake" which needs no Doctor
Freud, being the expression of a savage and guilt-ridden male
detumescence. I am told that to this day, Australian men are
forever killing the snake'.

I do not wish to wallow in the mud of Doctor Freud and his
followers' psychological tramplings but would just point out
that it would seem only common sense for this lady to attempt
to dispose of a critter such as the snake in question. I am told
that there are people who keep snakes as pets and in fact give
them the freedom of the house, but I have not met any.

Finally the paragraph ends with . . . 'The drover is absent
from the story, a point to be taken up later.' The point is indeed
taken up later with the words 'And we note that . . . there is no
drover. This is a reversal of situation, an inside-out truth, for we

know historically that there was a drover but there was historically no wife, not in any acceptable conventional sense.'

But of course there was no drover in the story. The title of the story is 'The Drover's *Wife*'. The drover was simply off somewhere droving and his wife remained at home. Just as there are many women today who keep the home together while their husbands are working in Antarctica or Papua New Guinea or simply in prison.

Henry Lawson was usually fair and even sympathetic in his attitude to Australian pioneer women, and did not mistake them for sheep, at least in his literature. Which is more than can be said for a mob of excited Italian students.

Bornia Park, NSW
(name withheld)

LETTER FROM CHINESE STUDENT

Wuhan University
April 14 1984

Respected Suzanne Kiernan,
How do you do? We are strangers to each other, so I should first briefly introduce myself to you. I'm a teacher at Wuhan University, who studied for two years at La Trobe University in Melbourne from 1980 to 1982.

Recently I read the leading magazine of Australia 'the *Bulletin*' in which I came across some problems I can't resolve by myself. That's why I'm writing this letter to you, and I sincerely hope you can give me reply (or the key to the questions I ask) at your earliest convenience. My questions arise from my reading of the following two passages (or notes by the editors):
1. 'Note: A number of European and American universities are now studying literature written in English from the former

colonies of the British Empire. This new literature from India, Africa, Canada, Malaysia, the Caribbean, the South Pacific, Papua New Guinea, New Zealand and Australia is known as Commonwealth literature.

'This is a transcription of a paper on Australian culture given, excitedly, by an Italian student Franco Casamaggiore, at a recent conference on Commonwealth Writing in Milan. It comes to us from writer Frank Moorhouse and we acknowledge also the inspired assistance of *Suzanne Kiernan* of the Department of Italian, University of Sydney.' (From 'the *Bulletin*', 29 January 1980, p.160.)

2. 'For the Bulletin Centenary Issue earlier this year, Frank Moorhouse supplied a transcript of a paper on Australian culture allegedly delivered by an Italian student , Franco Casamaggiore, to a conference on Commonwealth writing in Milan. The excitable Signor Casamaggiore outlined the implications of the Drover's Wife as seen by Henry Lawson, Russell Drysdale and Murray Bail. Here, Barbara Jefferis, journalist, author and former president of the Australian Society of Authors, presents the female side of the picture.' (From the *Bulletin*, 1980. 12. 23-30, p.156.)

Now I have four questions arising from the words underlined in red to ask:

1. What does 'transcription' mean? Does it mean 'translation from Italian to English' or ' a mere copy in the same language'?
2. What does 'excitedly' or 'excitable' mean? Why did the editor say Franco Casamaggiore is 'excitable' or 'excited'?
3. Does 'student' mean 'a person who's studying at school(s) and not yet a graduate'? or 'a scholar' or 'a person who's a researcher'?
4. Why is the word 'allegedly' used? Are the words in the first quoted passage true or not?

Best wishes to you
from Guo Zhuzhang

The University of Sydney
Sydney 2006
New South Wales
Australia

Department of Italian
11 May 1984

Dear Guo Zhuzhang,

I was very interested to receive your letter in which you ask me
if I can throw some light on problems you have encountered in
the matter of a piece of writing attributed to one Franco
Casamaggiore in the *Bulletin*.

I think I should tell you what I believe you already suspect –
that this is a joke on the part of the writer Frank Moorhouse,
whose name has been 'Italianised' (with a little semantic
liberty) to become 'Franco Casamaggiore'. This was the full
extent of what was described as my 'inspired assistance' in the
introductory remarks, which are the author's own, and are part
of the fiction. (In Italian, 'casa' = 'house', and 'maggiore' =
'more' – homophonous with 'moor', while not, of course,
having the same meaning.)

The use of the words 'excitedly' and 'inspired' which you
single out in the original story by Frank Moorhouse has the
function of signalling to the reader that the writer's intention is
ironic and satiric, and that what follows is not necessarily to be
taken at face value. The (pseudo) information that the story
'comes to us from writer Frank Moorhouse' is knowingly
ambiguous, since it could mean that he is simply transmitting it
from another source, or that it 'comes from' him in that he is its
originator.

Thus the story by Frank Moorhouse isn't a literary hoax in
the manner of the famous 'Ern Malley' case (which as a scholar

THE DROVER'S WIFE   113

of Australian letters you will doubtless be familiar with), but a joke, whose intention is to amuse rather than deceive. And Barbara Jefferis's use of the word 'allegedly' in her rejoinder to the original story indicates that she wishes to write in the same spirit of fun.

Although I teach in a Department of Italian, my interest in Australian literature is by no means secondary, and I would be very interested to hear at some future date about what you are doing in Australian studies at Wuhan University.

With best wishes,
Suzanne Kiernan

ITEM IN THE NATIONAL TIMES

FEARLESS FRANCO

SOMEONE should take a close look at the sort of cultural exports Foreign Affairs spends its money on.

At a literature conference at Wellington, New Zealand, this week, Franco Casa Moora, a self-styled Italian expert on Oz lit whose junket was funded by Foreign Affairs, delivered a paper suggesting that "sheep guilt" was the dominant sort of imagery in Australian literature.

He explained to the New Zealanders that because Australia had had no women for the first 50 years after colonisation, an intimate bond had developed between Australian males and the nation's sheep – aided by a technique of placing the sheep's rear legs in gumboots.

The "sheep guilt" had surfaced first in works such as Henry Lawson's The Drover's Wife. The eponymous wife, Casa Moora explained, was in reality a sheep.

The New Zealanders, having a high sheep population themselves, received the paper in anxious silence.

BULLETIN COVER

PATRICK COOK CARTOON, NATIONAL TIMES, APRIL 13-19, 1980

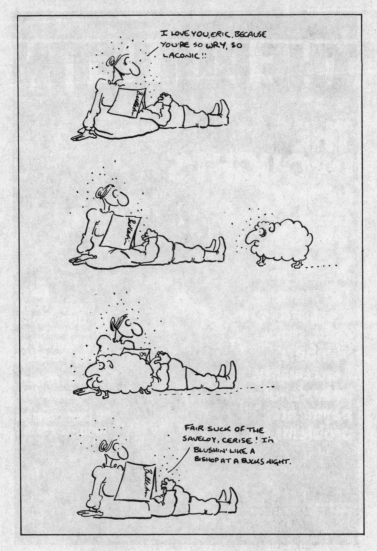

HOBBIES AND RECREATIONS, PLEASE STATE,
OR ON HOLIDAY WITH ROLAND BARTHES

Chief, I say to you that I am scratching for something to write about and you say why don't I write about my hobbies and recreation. You're kidding? Why not ask me to write about my 'honours and decorations'? I don't have hobbies and recreations, I just have nervous collapses. That's my only recreation – nervous collapse. Nervous collapse occurs at first because you don't have hobbies and recreations, but after a while the nervous collapse becomes something of a hobby. At first they occur because writers can spend two years or more working on a book which will be a disaster without anyone knowing this, including oneself. And then, a lot of the time when you think you're writing great literature you're really having a nervous collapse. The distinction between a nervous collapse and being a great artist is thin (on a day-to-day basis). And it's like one view of the Third World War – that it started the day the Second World War stopped. Nervous collapses are a little like that. But I can pick them now. When I cry at the silhouette of building cranes against the sunset, or when I find myself sitting without answering the telephone and it rings at a great distance, or when I put a cassette on the telephone answering machine saying that I have 'gone away for a year', or when I find myself saying a lot, 'that wasn't a very zen thing to do' – any of these signals indicate that I'm having, or am about to have, a nervous collapse.

When you're having a nervous collapse you can't really make travel arrangements or decisions of any kind. You have to stumble into a hole and recover without elaborate plans. That's the trick.

I usually book straight into the Hilton here in Sydney and sit watching the midday movies. (One day I'll tell you why I don't go to stay with friends of friends.) Handling the menu can be a giant undertaking, though, when you're having a collapse. Deciding when to eat and what to eat when you're alone and collapsed is sometimes almost beyond your capacity. My method is to start at the top of the menu and eat my way down. Once in New York while waiting for a film director to arrive to talk about a movie I had a nervous collapse. He was three weeks late and the hotel bill was ticking over like a water meter. I had a lot of trouble deciding when and what to eat there. If you use room service in New York you end up getting your breakfast for lunch and you lunch for afternoon tea and so on which contributes to nervous collapse. You're asleep when your dinner arrives.

In New York I went out from my hotel into Forty-fourth Street turned right and began daily to eat my way around the block (as long as they took American Express – I had no cash). Again, I began at the top of the menu in each restaurant. But the good thing about using room service a lot is that you eventually get to play cards with the staff.

If you book into your hometown Hilton you can telephone selected friends who never fail to come because they're curious to see you having a nervous collapse and to try room service. But it's good, too, because you are surrounded by foreigners and you can forget that you're still in Australia.

During a nervous collapse I become an expert for a month on all sorts of subjects. I hoard books ready for nervous collapses. I usually hoard books on one subject – say the history of the *Pall Mall Gazette*. When I retreat to a Hilton I take my hoard of books on one subject and read my way through them. But I find the knowledge stays with me for only about a month and anyhow none of my friends are interested in the subject, usually.

Usually the books relate to a fantasy I have about what I would like to have been other than a writer. Arun Joshi the Hindu writer once said to me that while it is good to write it is better still never to have needed to write. In fact, I would rather have been the editor of the *Pall Mall Gazette* in the last century. Or a colonel at Gallipoli.

Another approach to the collapse is to rent a car. A rented car is important because it disconnects you from your life. Your own car will be an ever-present reminder of your life – the hair pins, the registration due next month, that friction coming from the transmission, unanswered letters on the back seat. In a rented car, as one of my characters once observed, 'You are free of the bonds of ownership. The rented car is not your ego, rusting away, corroding, scratched, dented. A rented car renews itself at each renting and renews you with it. Certain things can be best and freely used when not owned.' (*Tales of Mystery and Romance*, Angus & Robertson, $5.95)

But you must only drive on country roads very slowly, drinking Heineken beer out of an esky in the back, and listening to country-and-western music.

The country-and-western music is important to the therapy because it will help you cry a lot. It will give you a vastly distorted view of reality, which also helps. For a time you will believe there are basic values to life and the only things which matter are children and watermelon wine. It is later, back in the real reality, that you realise that you've never seen let alone tasted, watermelon wine and that it doesn't sound all that appealing. And that the drug addicts who break into your flat every six months or so, break the newly planted trees in the street and smash bottles in the sand at the beach are 'children'.

Aimless country roads driving is good for you. I sometimes throw the shotgun into the back, camp at night, and shoot a rabbit or quail to cook on the camp fire. You get to pretend you're Karen Blixen.

Backpacking into the bush is OK but it's dangerous to go into the bush alone when having a nervous collapse. You may decide not to come back. And your map and compass work becomes a trifle sloppy. Or you sit under a gum tree and drink the whole of the five days booze and eat the chocolate provisioning.

I have trouble, though, finding a friend to go into the bush with me because my friends are sybarites and lounge lizards.

People also say behind my back that I'm a zealot and that I walk X kilometres a day and that I have strict rules on camp hygiene and do not open the bar until sunset, and so on. Some of the things they say are true – I keep a very detailed log book – and I fancy myself at bush medicine, including a little surgery.

But if you're having a collapse and go into the bush you hear voices too, which doesn't help. I hear bad songs, badly sung. It's best to stick to rented cars, country music, and backroads.

I once used opera as a place to go. Another world. But it's about time I said publicly that I failed Opera (on the back of some of my books it lists opera as my 'recreation' – in those days I was anxious to be able to supply answers to questions about my 'hobbies and recreations' and 'honours and decorations').

I subscribed to *Opera Australia* for four years. I passed Opera I because that's easy. For a country boy like myself opera is breathtaking and it's a thousand miles from Balmain and my life. That gets you through year one. Opera II is harder but you do start to recognise the tunes and by now you've read twenty opera program notes at least. But, by Opera II, you've seen through the dazzle and find the stories very silly and that opera is not about the stories. By Opera III you find that it's not the tunes you're supposed to be listening for but the singing, in particular it's not the music really, but the singer's performance on that particular night compared with the other singers' performances on other particular nights. What makes Opera III more difficult is that people like Patrick White, Gough Whitlam, Margaret Whitlam, the Kerrs, David Gyger, see you at the Opera Theatre bar and at interval seek your opinion. In Opera III you're expected to have an opinion. You can't forever say 'that it's breathtaking, and for a country boy, etc.' (I now listen to opera only in the bush after backpacking. That way I can skip the story, get the singing and the tunes and avoid the quizzing by experts at the bar.) But really, I have to say I failed Opera.

Once, if the collapse coincided with the Film Festival you could book into the Hilton and walk down to the Festival at 9.30 a.m. and watch movies until midnight for two weeks. You could sneak in after the lights went down and out before they came up, to avoid ex-lovers. You could go back to your room at the Hilton and watch the late movies if you wanted and have a bottle of bourbon sent up on room service. But now I find that the Film Festival films are selected on whether they worry the middle classes or not. These days the more worried the film the better for the film festival in Sydney. The selectors don't seem too happy unless they're worried. This is no good for someone who is middle class and having a collapse. So I suggest just staying in the Hilton and watching television and playing cards with the staff.

CONVALESCENCE
....

The dirty kitchen was the headquarters of her dirty personality: a gas stove with a grease cosmetic, an ulcerated porcelain sink, a wooden drying board greasy to the touch, a refrigerator smelling of perishing rubber, burning carbon from the motor, decaying food, odorous containers, shells and carcasses of insects under the refrigerator, and the bottom shelf having a dark, congealed stain which looked as if it had seeped from a wound, and which he called privately, every time he opened the refrigerator, 'refrigerator blood'. He was having a nervous breakdown and had been ejected from his domestic home, low on funds, and someone, a so-called friend, had arranged for him to have a room in this house. He was a non-paying guest unable to make other arrangements for himself, a slumped and bruised psyche. He had no rights in the house but on the other hand, no responsibilities. When he had first focused on the kitchen he was too exhausted and personally defeated to clean it himself, but then lying tranquilised on his bed in the attic room he concluded that he had no 'right' to clean it even if he had had the energy. That it would be some sort of infringement of her living style, an implied comment on her as a person, if not a pointed and insulting criticism of her hygiene, an offence to her hospitality, and a 'statement', worse, about him and his obsessiveness.

Jesus, he thought, I'm trapped with that kitchen. I can't make a move. His estimation of the age of the accumulated filth in the kitchen, his carbon-dating of it, by examining the carcasses of insects, the expiry dates on packets, was that it had been like that for three years. It had been building up like that for at least three years. She was only 30. It was not the result of senility or palsy. She was not crippled with arthritis.

All he could manage with the kitchen was to have coffee. He bought his own cup, stirred it with his own teaspoon, used his own instant coffee (being too defeated to begin to reassemble the elaborate coffee-making equipment which had been lost in the domestic warfare). He took to placing a sheet of white, A4 paper on the sink and putting his cup and teaspoon on it. He replaced the A4 every two days. This was his only use, his only visit to the place. She used it for making nothing else, it seemed, than toasted sandwiches. He could not believe that three year of toasted sandwiches could produce such decay and domestic rubble.

He had smelled the unmistakeable smell of toasted sandwiches and had observed her on the rare occasions that they crossed tracks in the house. She was 'considerate' and did not make social demands on him.

She lived on toasted sandwiches. He'd always considered the smell of toasted bread homely. But she changed it to a smell of domestic wretchedness. It was the poverty of her imagination as a person, the absence of flair, and a carelessness about her diet that began to be represented by the smell of toasting bread from that squalid kitchen.

She did sometimes call to him, offering him a toasted sandwich. He always declined with a polite, appreciative voice which concealed a raging repugnance.

He would lie on his bed, tranquilised, just sufficiently, he realised, to prevent his repugnance towards her from screaming out. He began to form in his mind a map of her household and her bodily function. He used a poetry of naming learned from army map-reading – polluted-creek, old-dump, disused-well, swampy ground, unexploded shells.

He called her respiratory system the 'polluted creek'. She had a congenital congestion of the nose and lungs – a chronic sinusitis. She hawked too, from cigarette smoking, like a sick cat. He had at first tolerated it by telling himself that it was a seasonal cold. But they passed from one season to another and it persisted. He realised it was a permanent congestion and it would always be heard through the house like strained plumbing in an old hotel.

On the occasions when there was obligatory conversation – standing around pretending to be chatting in her kitchen, he trying not to rest his hand on any of the surfaces – this permanent congestion would not only punctuate her chat, but he found that she also examined her soggy tissue for the results of her effort. Maybe the doctor had advised her to watch for blood. He would, of course, look away, but he found it optically compelling and his fringe vision would still watch her do it.

In the second week or so he tried to joke her into an awareness of the impoliteness or vulgarity of her action. He said that his grandfather had called looking into one's phlegm 'gold mining'.

To his horror, she took the joking to be an acceptance of the behaviour – as a shared, if not intimacy, then domestic playfulness.

She would push her tissue at him, laughing, saying 'Here, like to fossick around?'

So he would lie on his bed of nerve nails high in the house, hearing her hawking and blowing her nose and inescapably, no matter how much he concentrated on other things, or tried to read, inescapably a laughing image of her would be before him thrusting a sodden tissue at him, screaming, 'Here, like to fossick around?' He suspected that it was a gesture of domestic closeness intended to make him at ease and to make him feel he belonged. Oh, Jesus.

She cleaned her ears too much. He found ear-wax stained cotton 'buds' – he found the word 'bud' so ill-used that that too became repulsive, as though one took, say, rose buds and cleaned one's nostrils or ears or whatever. He found these cotton-wad sticks browned like used toilet tissue, he found them everywhere, but always at the telephone. When she called to him, 'Phone – for you!' he would clamber downstairs from his dim room knowing, knowing, and wanting to cry, that there would be a wax-stained cotton-wad stick somewhere near the telephone which was in the dark hall.

In the first few days at her place, in the dark hall, called to the telephone, he had put his hand accidentally on the cotton-wad, wax-stained. He had felt the soft, near wetness while engaging with the voice on the telephone, and consequently with only part attention, had removed whatever it was that was sticking to his palm. The first time he could hardly believe it and had removed it with a visceral spasm of distaste. He thought it was an aberration on her part. But it happened again. And again. He concluded that she sat at the telephone cleaning her ears, or whatever part of her body the cotton-wadded sticks would enter. When she called, 'Phone – for you!', he would go down knowing that he had to watch out for these things which could be on the telephone table, on the stool, or in some unexpected place. He now always remembered to take a clean tissue, to pick them up and throw them somewhere down the dark hallway to fall onto the dark, dirty carpet along with whatever else had accumulated there. That was none of his business, that part of the house. Indeed, nowhere but his room was properly and technically 'part of his business'.

In his map of her house and personality he called these wax-stained, or whatever-stained, cotton-wad sticks, 'landmines'.

She didn't clean, but instead trusted heavily in vermin

powder. She sprinkled this toxic powder about the house, with irresponsible abandon.

But she never removed the kill. The body count was obvious, but she left them. He was intrigued to see that they did eventually disappear, either eaten by other insects or by decomposition into dust.

Maybe she liked the carcasses around as evidence of her good and effective work. Or as trophies. He called these 'enemy dead'.

The sodden, or at least *used* tissues were everywhere in the house, like turds.

She did not wear new clothes, but always bought second-hand ones. Maybe this was a clever 'style' thing to do, but he found that, because of her personality and habits, the old clothes she bought became as repugnant and as frightening as a shroud. As they stood 'chatting' in the kitchen, he standing well clear of any fixture, the clothing would inflame his imagination.

He could not stop himself seeing the old bodies which had inhabited the clothing before she had bought it. She would say 'this is a real find'. She would twirl around in some dress from the 1940s. He would see the old women's bodies which had left their deposits in the clothing. His mind would, like some forensic scientist, examine the fabric under a microscope of nausea, the evidence of blood, of menstruation, of disease, of vomit, of urine, of excreta, of saliva, of phlegm. Of how many owners before her?

'Chic?' she would say, holding the dress to her body, proudly. Her underwear also came from second-hand shops.

'Feel the quality of this silk,' she would say, holding out to him some second-, third-, two-hundredth-hand slip or bra.

She would in this way force him to touch the material.

When his birthday arrived like a gloomy, bored friend, he expected that no one would remember. Nor did he care. But one of his friends must have mentioned it to her, in the interests of his morale.

In the interests of his morale, she cooked him a cake. Cooked it in the vermin-littered, toxic-powdered, greasy kitchen.

When she called him to the kitchen and he saw her spreading icing on the cake, he knew that was what he could smell that was different in the house. For the first time, it was not a toasted sandwich, but it hadn't been all cake-smell either.

The cake was sitting on the wooden cutting board, danger-ously close to a piece of rusted steel-wool. He had a vision of a piece of rusted, food-speck-encrusted steel wool accidentally being baked in her cake.

The cake looked fly specked. Flies drifted around the kitchen untouched by the toxic vermin-powder.

'I'm touched,' he said, 'I'm very touched.'

The oven door was open and he could see for the first time into the oven, the fatty deposits of years of cooking burned into the walls of the oven. At least, he thought, the heat would have killed some of the bacteria.

She began to cut it. He realised that of course, he would have to eat it.

'I don't – it sounds silly – but I can't eat cake.'

The smell of the cooking cake had not been all cake smell because the rarely used oven had had to burn off its residue of past bakings, and roastings. The fatty decay had to be burned off and had filled the house. He could now identify the smell that pervaded the house, displacing the toasted and burnt-bread smell that was its characteristic smell.

The cake was probably imbued with the burnt rot of all that had passed through the sleazy oven.

'You can't eat cake!' she obviously disbelieved him. 'But you are the first man I've cooked a cake for.'

'I'm sorry – I'm thrilled – but I can't.'

'Come on,' she said, 'just a mouthful.'

She cut a slice with a dirty knife, which he saw was corroded, not the blade so much, as the imitation bone handle, the bone had corroded away from the knife blade revealing an ugly spine, like a gangrenous fracture.

She held it out to him, the slice wobbling on the blade of the knife, holding it steady with her fingers.

'She broke off a piece and put it in her mouth, salivating, he thought, quite heavily. Her saliva-wet fingers returned to the slice of cake and broke off a piece, 'mmmmmmmm, quite delicious, even if I say so myself.'

'I can't honestly eat cake. It's an allergy.'

'Nonsense – here,' she pushed the piece held in her saliva-wet fingers towards his mouth, and he reared back.

'No, I've never eaten cake.'

'You eat biscuits – I've seen you eating biscuits. Worse, I've seen you smuggling packets of biscuits into your room. Bingeing.'

'No. Please.'

She was backing him across the kitchen, part of his mind was hysterically avoiding contact with the kitchen and the other part hysterically moving from the menace of the filthy cake.

'I'm not a well person.'

'A teensy piece of cake on your birthday will do wonders for your morale. Every person deserves at least that – a birthday cake.'

She must have thought he was being 'playful'.

She darted at him with the cake piece held in her fingers.

He weaved like a boxer.

'Please stop!'

'I think baby wants to be fed by mama.'

He had gone around the kitchen table once, once had put his hand on the kitchen table and pulled it away as if bitten, glancing at it to see how it had been contaminated, moving all the while away from her advancing fingers. She finally grabbed him and, laughing, forced the cake into his partly closed mouth, some of it getting onto his tongue. He gagged.

She pulled back from him, a bit shaken by the genuineness of the gagging.

He coughed.

'Please stop.' He staggered from the kitchen into the small backyard, and spat out the cake.

'You're serious,' she said, following him.

'Yes. I can't eat cake.'

'I'm sorry. I thought you were playing. Never mind. I'll eat it up.'

One night, rigid with insomnia and torment from all the wrong he'd done people and himself, his mind roved the house and poked its nose into all its foul corners.

The mind came back to his room having made a nauseous tour of the dark decay of the house and its mistress.

The mind stopped at the bed and the mattress and for the first time wondered about the mattress. The sheets and blankets were his, but not the mattress.

Next day, he asked her outright whether the mattress was second hand.

She was bemused by the question, thought, and said, 'No, the mattress in your room is not second hand. It's my old mattress.'

'Your old mattress.'

'Yes from my childhood.'

He must have gone pale and perhaps rocked slightly.

'I slept on that mattress for twenty-five years.'

Before his mind, in a foul gust, swept the years of bed-wetting, years of her menstruating, the colds and running noses, the sweatings of the night fever, the festering of childhood sores, the weeping of wounds, the dirty hair, the dirty feet, the whole mess of excretions which had seeped down into the mattress over those years.

He left the house that day, without a word, to stay at a Hilton.

'Nothing ennobles me,' Wesley said, at the refrigerator, 'not demonstrations, not folk music, not handing out how-to-vote cards, and certainly not this Wake for Jack Kerouac.'

Around us the Wake stormed for Jack Kerouac.

'And I shouldn't be here,' I said, 'but anyhow ennoblement isn't a sensation which an Australian should expect to experience.'

'I guess not,' she said, 'but at least you can record your observation of the Wake.'

'I'm more inclined to agree with your brother,' I said, 'that it is difficult to understand why people write anything but fiction, seeing that the truth is impossible.'

'Did he say that?'

We nodded at Nigel, who smiled, said something we couldn't catch, whinnied, and inhaled himself into a joint.

'I should be here,' Wesley said, 'when you consider the state of my relations with Milton.'

'There's your brother,' I said, pointing with the toe of my shoe towards Wesley's brother across the room.

'I bet half of them don't know who Jack Kerouac was,' Wesley said, propped against the refrigerator. The refrigerator was continually being opened to reveal a well-lit but empty stage.

Wesley's brother, 'the writer', came over and said he and Milton were now 'working off each other' rather than working 'against each other's fictions.'

He said it was the beginning of communalised literature.

'How does it operate?' I enquired, having been trained by my father to ask questions rather than to give answers.

'It operates this way,' said Wesley's brother. 'Milton tells me over the telephone a key sentence from a story he is writing. I make a response to this key sentence while at the same time reacting 'fictionally' on my typewriter there and then. You see my reaction on the phone orally is an 'event', that is, voice-to-voice in the oral tradition, I then telephone Carmel and initiate an 'event' by telling her what I've written and she reacts to that and responds to it and then telephones Milton who writes some more and then telephones me. We are working with fictional representations of each other at the same time, you see. Of course, I know what you are going to say – the 'real' story is the uncaptured parts of the linked telephone calls – the parts we don't think of putting down, or cannot 'catch' as it were, in flight because the spontaneous interaction is too quick to be consciously observed and recorded.'

No, I thought, no I wasn't going to say that, but I was able to say, 'It is recorded though – ' winking an academic smile, 'by ASIO.'

'God yes!' Wesley's brother was excited, 'of course! ASIO must have the only complete oral history of the Australian Left. Richard Hall must get the tapes for us.'

'And the Labor governments have made the only oral history of the Australian Right. We were in danger of losing that.'

'We're working towards the private story also, Milton and I, the story for a readership of, say twenty people, each of whom participates in the making of the story by telephone, and who alone know the story. Cabbala.'

Wesley's brother, over-excited by his ideas, trailed off into private thought.

'Telephone, telephone?' said Bunny Stockwell Anderson of the English Department, lurching past, 'someway one the telephone,' he said.

We turned our uncomprehending stares at him. He had taken off his shoes and was walking through the Wake, immaculately dressed, as always, from Hunts, but without shoes. A reference I thought, perhaps, to Jack Kerouac. He took the uncomprehending stares and said, 'Ooopsy' and passed by.

Milton came over to us at the refrigerator and said, like a notice, 'Keep the Door of the Refrigerator shut at All Times.'

'But there is nothing in the refrigerator,' I said.

'It costs money – it burns up ohms,' said Milton.

'Since when have you been Guardian of the Ohm,' Wesley quipped. Lying behind her joke, of course, was the fact that Milton and she had lived together for some unsatisfactory period when he had been pursuing the 'domestic mode'.

He was now allegedly having an affair with her brother, although this was dismissed by some as his attempt to create the appearance, at least, of his capacity to enter the darker worlds of sexuality.

'Amps,' I corrected, suddenly unsure, 'it's amps which are burned, isn't it, not ohms.'

'Our lady of the Amps perhaps,' Wesley said, 'Vamps.'

'We're going to get the ASIO tapes,' Wesley's brother exclaimed to Milton, putting his arm around him, 'Richard Hall will get them for us – for the cassette magazine.'

Milton said that he thought they should incorporate what people said about the stories into the later versions of the stories.

'Who actually writes the story?' I asked, not having their speed.

'We all do,' they said together, turning to each other and giving a small bow.

Wesley made a vomiting gesture.

'We are communally tilling the literary acreage,' Milton said.

'Sounds more like the destruction of Vietnam to me,' Wesley said, and continued 'never before have more explosives, napalm and concentrated artillery fire been turned on such a small innocent, and agriculturally worthless piece of landscape.'

'Go over the same ground until it speaks to you,' said Wesley's brother.

'Charcot to Freud,' Milton completed.

'He didn't mean that you should make the ground uninhabitable,' Wesley said.

They moved off, Milton propelling Wesley's brother away.

Wesley gave the Sicilian cursing gesture with her forearm, and a Greek spit.

'Winsome couple,' she observed.

What happened next was this. They were linked there, arm in arm, trying to do a vaudeville routine while at the same time drinking from a common glass, when for absolutely no reason, Milton said, 'The way to tame an eagle is to keep him tired.'

I was about to rejoin, across the room, for I was still tuned, as it were, to them, straining as always to be part of it, feeling always some distance from the centre, I was about to say in response to Milton, 'Eagles catch no flies.' I am something of a student of folklore. This proverb means that people with the stature of eagles do not concern themselves with trivia.

I was about to say this, across the kitchen, throwing it to Milton, the way you return in a conversation knowing that there is no 'logical' answer, required, and that in the absence of witty response you can say something which is at least parallel

to the first statement and which may perhaps catch onto,
release, some unforeseen wit, an unforeseen humorous association (seen sometimes by one's unconscious, but not 'seen' by
the speaker until spoken). If delivered with appropriate swag-
ger it passes for wit.

Wesley's brother, however, ignored the game-playing conversation with a moody toss and said to Milton urgently, 'What
did you say that for?'

Milton repeated, 'The way to tame an eagle is to keep him
tired.' Having, I think sensed that it was 'alive' for Wesley's
brother, and determined to play it through.

Wesley's brother pulled away from Milton, his face alert
with tension.

'What's bugging you?' Milton said to Wesley's brother.

'Why did you say that!' Wesley's brother again demanded,
obviously disturbed.

I felt I was looking in the window on the adjoining flats.

'It's true – the way you tame an eagle is to keep him tired.'

'Don't keep saying it!' Wesley's brother screamed, throwing
the glass to the floor.

'That's one of our good glasses,' Milton said peevishly.

'Oh dear,' said Wesley.

'Someone's playing games with me and I don't like it,'
Wesley's brother said, standing away not only from Milton,
but from us all, staring from one face to another angrily.

Wesley's brother is a robust sort of poet, but prone to
paranoia.

The misty, alcoholic glee had blown away from around us,
leaving behind a bright, fluorescent kitchen glare.

'It's not a game – the way you tame an eagle it to keep him
tired.'

I was surprised that Milton kept repeating the phrase when it
obviously was pressing on a nerve.

Wesley's brother screamed again, putting his hands over his
ears, 'Don't say that! Don't say that!'

'Anyone for telephones?' Bunny Stockwell Anderson said, soft-shoeing it, or soft-socking through the kitchen.

'Shut up,' said Wesley's brother.

I said, in an aside to Wesley, 'I think it all refers to Kerouac.'

'How?' she whispered back.

'I don't know,' I whispered.

'What about the ping pong ball?' Wesley's brother said with cold seriousness, all hysteria swallowed from his voice.

I laughed, jovially, thinking that he had characteristically turned the conversation on its head, a way of forcing Milton to grapple with a new play – to make him jump for the ball.

Wesley's brother turned to me and said, in answer to my laugh, that someone had been bouncing a ping-pong ball in the flat above his, keeping it up throughout the night in a steady beat, 'When I get out of bed and go up to the flat above to complain it stops. I go back to my flat and get into bed and it starts again.'

I was now feeling socially very slippery. I was trying to smile, yet not knowing whether a smile was appropriate or not. Or what sort of smile.

Still looking at me, but not really talking to me – talking really to Milton – he said, 'Item three – the bookcases.'

'Item three – the bookcases,' I said, involuntarily.

'Item three – the bookcases,' Wesley's brother said, emphasising the seriousness of his mood, 'the bookcases in the American's room – there was something very strange about it. I looked through the books, and although I couldn't name the titles, there were key titles missing.

'Key books were missing. While the American was in the lavatory I looked under his bed and there were books. He had removed certain books from the shelf to give me a certain impression. He wanted me to think x instead of y. These books were also missing from your shelves at the university.'

He turned to Milton with this accusation although I pointed a bemused questioning finger at myself as well.

'Someone is playing games with me,' Wesley's brother said, grimly.

We were all holding our glasses too tightly.

'I don't know this American,' said Milton, too calmly.

'Please,' said Wesley, not to any person, but as an undirected prayer.

'That is, I think, the whole point,' Wesley's brother said.

'Excuse me,' I said to Wesley's brother, 'I have to go . . . ' I gestured towards the lavatory, that safe place deep in the party somewhere.

'You stay,' he said curtly.

'The whole point of what?' Milton said.

'And I laid a false trail.'

'You laid a false trail?' I said involuntarily again, feeling compelled to say something, not to stand silent within a conversation. I am always compelled to end silences, too.

'I laid a false trail, I told Milton and the American that I was going to the opal fields for a few months. They were the only two I told. I then took a cab as far as Penrith and returned back to my flat. A thread I had attached to several items had been broken.

Nothing had been stolen, but someone had been in there – doing god knows what.'

'Paranoia,' said Milton.

'It would be paranoia if there was no pattern.'

'What is the pattern?'

'There is always a pattern,' I said 'except for basic matter.'

'Oh shut up,' said Milton, 'you are humouring him.'

Although I ask questions I am also somewhat compulsive in supplying answers to the questions, fearful lest I have asked a question of someone who does not have an answer.

'You want me to go back to the doctor?' Wesley's brother said.

'Why should I want that?' asked Milton.

'To have me in a drugged state – the way to tame an eagle is to keep him tired.'

I smiled because it seemed, fleetingly, to be a good answer.

'You're crazy,' Milton said to Wesley's brother.

Wesley's brother pushed Milton over, Milton fell on his backside on the kitchen lino tiles, spilling his wine.

Milton tried to get up and he pushed him over again.

'Get out of this house,' shouted Milton and Wesley's brother darkened, and then went off darkly out of the house.

'Shouldn't we, ah, do something?' I asked.

'Your brother sabotaged the readings tonight – he changed the date and place on all the notices at the University. No one turned up.'

'God what a rotten wake for Jack Kerouac.'

Milton back on his feet inspected his wine-stained clothing.

'Come to the bedroom while I change,' Milton said to Wesley, the invitation was loaded with meaning.

As they went off, they laughed, and I thought I heard Milton say, 'It worked,' but I could be wrong.

I noticed then that the door of the refrigerator was open, just an inch the sneaky light glinted out, and silently the refrigerator pumped chilled air into the almost deserted Wake for Jack Kerouac. When Milton and Wesley awoke in the morning they would be hoary with frost.

THE DEATH OF THE TELEGRAM
....

As you know Chief, I have a love for the dying art forms – the speech, the sermon, the motto, the letter to the editor (which I think is making a comeback), civic tributes and, of course, the telegram, which we now know is dying an agonising death.

I was invited to the Sydney College of the Arts to talk about something – I lost the letter – so I talked about The Death of the Telegram. The students were indulgent.

Firstly I told them about the novel not being dead. Everyone talks about The Death of the Novel – it had mourners in the nineteenth century (maybe that was what I was supposed to talk about). But I told them about a novel called *Gadsby* (not *Gatsby*) by Ernest Vincent Wright written in 1939 without using the letter 'e', except in the author's name. It could have been titled *The Story of E*. He did it to violate the statistical pattern of the English language without violating either grammar or sense. Which is a better reason for writing a novel than a lot I've heard. The queer thing is that if you didn't know it wasn't using 'e' you might not miss it. But it makes eerie reading when you do know. The absence of the 'e' creates a sense of deprivation – a letter-e deficiency. You need a shot of 'e' badly after reading even a part of the book and although you know that the author has not used an 'e' you still check each page trying to catch him out.

Part of the 'e' deficiency caused me, I think, to say that it was a 'queer' and 'eerie' experience to read it.

When I told the College of the Arts students about this I noticed that a few didn't laugh. I think they might have been working on the same idea.

The point is, I told them, that the novel is not dead – there are at least twenty-five other novels which could still be written.

Again the laughter was a little thin.

However, I went on, the telegram is dead – forget about it as an art form. The use of the domestic telegram had in fact been in decline since about 1935 as people overcame their inhibition about using the telephone for long-distance calls. Maybe the telephone conversation is the new art-form and I suggested they study police phone taps. Maybe this is where the crime novels are being written. They didn't think phone taps were a joke.

But it is not only the use of the telegram which has declined, I think the standard has declined. On the evidence of the telegrams I receive I don't think people sweat over the writing of the telegram the way they used to. A painter friend of mine, Adam Rish, puts a bit of effort into it. He's very good at one word telegrams but they can't be quoted because they require elaborate context. The telegram today is more verbose because affluent people don't try as hard to save money by eliminating unnecessary words. It was the elimination of unnecessary words which gave the telegram its force and vitality. My mother sweated over eliminating unnecessary words as a matter of pride.

The economy of telegrams can produce ambiguity. A journalist telegrammed the actor Cary Grant 'How old Cary Grant?' Grant telegrammed back 'Fine how you?'

At this point a few of the students excused themselves.

Hemingway was the first to realise that the telegram was an art form. He was perhaps the last of the great telegram writers. He exclaimed about cable-ese once, 'Isn't it a great language!' I don't know to whom he exclaimed this or what their reply was. He published two of his press cables unchanged as the short story *On the Quai at Smyrna*, and the story *Old Man at the Bridge* was an unchanged press cable. Or at least that's what Hemingway says. Maybe they are stories which were written to *read* like telegrams. Hemingway was a bit of a liar.

As a literary form Henry James played about with it in the story *The Cage*, where the action (?) takes place at a telegraph operator's 'cage' or office. Alphonse Allais wrote a story called *The Telegraph Operator* in which a gentleman falls in love with the girl in the telegraph office and goes as often as possible to send telegrams in hope of attracting her attention. But she remains professionally impersonal, as someone sending and receiving personal messages should be. He also fears that she might think him crazy for sending all those dozens of pointless messages to his friends. Finally he hits on the answer and sends a telegram to a friend saying 'I am madly in love with the little red-haired telegraph operator at Baisenmoyen-Cert.'

But even the joking telegram seems to have declined except for tired wedding jokes. I'm not impressed with singing telegrams or gorilla-grams – they seem to be a way of avoiding the hard work of actually creating a funny telegram.

In the 1930s when a group of Oxford undergraduates heard that Kipling received 10 shillings a word for his short stories they telegrammed him 10 shillings and asked for 'one of his best words.' He telegramed back 'thanks' (even that's not *really* so funny, Rudyard). You can telegram money, which I'd forgotten. They are better telegrams than a joking gram.

It's difficult to recall joking telegrams. Dorothy Parker sent a telegram to a friend on the birth of the friend's child, 'We all knew you had it in you.' Dorothy, you've done better than that.

Hollywood liked the telegram. When MGM fired William Faulkner as script writer they did it by telegram. The director Howard Hawkes wired back, 'You can't sack Faulkner. He's America's greatest writer.' MGM wired back 'You're fired too.'

Maybe funny telegrams are like *Punch* cartoons – they never were as funny as you remember.

A few more students left the talk.

But the point of the talk was supposed to be that if a technology is on its way out nothing will make people use it.

We use the telegram, but the telex is taking its place. The telegram used to be the way to get the attention of people at the other end. To get them to jump. A telex is used that way now. Or a courier. Which is really a reversion to an older technology called 'the messenger'.

The Australian film industry discovered the courier. Even though film projects take years to develop, every step in that development is carried out with dramatic urgency and all communication cannot wait for the ordinary mails, but must be rushed across the city or the nation by breathless express couriers.

A visit from a courier is a bit like receiving a present.

Some legal and important mail, I've noticed, is now sent like a telegram, with something of the drama of the telegram.

The letters are delivered by courier, but are delivered *flat*, sandwiched between inflexible cardboard so that they cannot be folded or bent – and you get the letter uncreased like some proclamation.

But if more of our telephone calls are to be recorded by security agencies and eventually find their way into courts, history books, the news media, maybe we should pay attention to the style as well as the content. It could unintentionally lead to a vast improvement in the standard of telephone calls.

The two remaining students clapped politely.

DISCUSSION OF THE SUBJECT OF DEATH

IS NOW CONCLUDED (A FOUND STORY)

How the hell do you write an obituary that is halfways acceptable for a man whom you've known for quite a while, worked with, yet did not greatly admire, on a paper where we try to tell it as it is?

That's my problem.

I was the only senior staffer on duty when the news came through, Young Morris came back from the telephone and said, 'Berry Tonge has knocked himself off.'

I told him to go away and check it because it sounded to me like a hoaxer from Stewart's because, whatever else you might have to say or not say about Berry Tonge, he is definitely Life Affirmative.

Young Morris came back after having rung the widow and said that it was no hoax alright.

I was infuriated. I think I am entitled to self-destruct whenever I choose, but I would never do it so close to deadline, which again struck me as rather comic because Berry Tonge always put himself forward as a considerate person.

Berry Tonge wrote a column for us (this is the beginning of the Obituary proper) before we went down-market and found readership. Down-market I often sayeth to Tonge is where most of humanity lives. He never listened to me and that is probably why he is where he is now. In the morgue.

Well, he wrote a column for us even after we went down-market in search of readership, and the column was, as you all should know, called *Life Stylish*. I always said to Tonge, 'Berry I don't have a life style, I just have life.' He ignored me as usual. His last piece for us was 'Listening to the Silence' (Jan 3). Don't rush away – you can read it later.

Now I was not one of those who admired his writing or, let it all hang out, his ideas. But I'm the only one here in the office and it's forty-five minutes to deadline. Many of our readers, however, did commend him for his Earth Philosophy. Young Morris has found fourteen congratulatory letters in the twenty-seven months during which Berry Tonge wrote sixty-one pieces for us (when you have nothing to say use some statistics). I want to be honest, as he would, I hope, wish me to be. Berry your Earth Philosophy got up my nostril.

But I suppose the virility symbol he wore on a chain around his neck, his knee boots, his kaftans, and his home-grown tomatoes were just not my style. I come from the anonymous sartorial style of the crumpled, cheapsuit journalism, albeit, one trying to make it into the New Journalism and keep a job.

But I think it was that he worried about those two things we cannot afford to worry about, immortality through achievement and Proper Report. Berry Tonge did not claim to be a writer (to his credit), but saw himself, rather, as a Teacher in the older sense. The Old Teaching. His expression to be precise was 'A Free Teacher'. He would not work within the system or for an institution. He wanted to be Respected as a Free Teacher by the world and kept for it and remembered for it. Well, Berry, here I am thirty-five minutes to deadline trying to write the only obituary you'll get, I'm afraid. Bad luck. Hard cheese. You were never very strong in irony, were you Berry? You'll excuse me while I take a small swig from the office bottle. Ah. Yes.

You asked a lot of the world, Berry. You become very vulnerable to the world when you demand such things. I myself wouldn't dream of asking the world for these things. My life is based on one question which I live with most mornings of my life. That question is 'How have the sub-editors fucked up my story this time?'

People will now question, of course, how you could write sixty-one columns on the Richness of Life and still do away with yourself. There was not one column on suicide that I can see, now leafing through. How come? You were supposed to be telling it as is, you were the last Flower Child. You were still using the jargon which Young Morris would have to look up in a glossary of Hippie Terminology. Methinks, Berry, you were not letting everything hang out. Those columns were again part of the world's rich bullshit.

I'll put it another way, Berry, I think, you silly old bugger, that last night you re-read some of the things you wrote, I hope while sipping elderberry wine, or whatever your tipple was, if you tippled, and in one moment of blinding clarity you saw that you didn't believe in it, and the world wasn't listening. The world was never going to join the Movement.

Young Morris points out to me that this is our first obituary in sixty-two months of publication. I've taught Young Morris to collect facts.

I've found something now that I can respect you for, Berry. If you did in fact have this one rare moment of blinding clarity and have made the ultimate response to self-knowledge, I salute you.

What I really suspect is that you were making a final manoeuvre for immortality. I suspect you were using the ultimate act to try to extract from life Proper Respect. No go, Berry. It didn't work.

Goodbye you poor bastard. Ten minutes to deadline. Blase.

Notes: Morris says that Berry Tonge OD'd on twenty-eight

sleeping capsules at 2.23 a.m. and was d.o.a. at Prince Alfred. Good work, Morris.

LETTERS, MARCH 13

'Sirs, It is customary on a newspaper that the person who writes the obituary should have some understanding of the life about which he has taken upon himself to write.

'We the undersigned wish to express our dismay at the disrespectful, frivolous and unfair obituary by Blase (March 6).

'On one point, however, the obituary was correct – Berry Tonge was a Teacher. His pieces in your journal were often regretted by his friends as a departure from his vocation and suffered from the influences which swirl around such newspapers, no matter how hard one fights them. You would be described as one of such influences – negative and destructive and soured.

'You fail to mention his books or his past great project, *The Commonplace Book of Key Insights*.

'He sought a better understanding of the psychological mechanisms of human growth and the possibility of transcendence through flexible love. This made him queer among the happy ego-trippers who make up the staff of your newspaper and who seemed to him to be in an extended adolescence. He admitted to close friends that he had failed to find self-transcendence through flexible love and to have any impact at all on the staff of the newspaper, especially during November and December of last year. Of course, none of you noticed. There was a circle of beneficent influence directing its beam at your newspaper, under the guidance of Berry Tonge, but this could not penetrate the soullessness of your scene. We pity Young Morris and our heart goes out to him.

'A point of fact: Berry did not wear a "virility symbol" around his neck, it was a "fecundity" symbol and expressed

more than Blase could understand or deal with in thirteen
paragraphs on page 40.

'Berry's relationship to sperm was a thousand miles away
from concepts of "virility" and, although there is ample
testament to his virility, he said many times that it meant
nothing to him. Fecundity may be the outcome of mature
virility correctly applied in the service of transcendent flexible
love.

'As to the Why. He was very deeply demoralised by his
efforts at the newspaper both to involve your readers and to
turn around the minds of those like yourself who worked there.
For over a year, week in and week out, he not only wrote the
column but delivered it in person to you at the newspaper,
hoping that his presence in the office would ultimately have its
effect. It might have helped you if you'd eaten those home-
grown tomatoes and other gifts from the soul of a very soulful
man. But oh no – not for you the cynic.'

Signed, 7 of Berry Tonge's friends

'Sirs,
For Berry Tonge
I heard a horde of people
asking why
and yet for some
it was just a case
of time
and place
he spoke about it
once or twice
and someone said
he'd never have the guts
but then he saw a last defiant chance
to swing the wheel of destiny
and grasped it firmly

yet all he lacked was love
from those he loved the most'

Another friend.

'Sirs, What was the last insight in Berry Tonge's Commonplace Book of Key Insights?
　'Perhaps the indefatigable Morris could dig it up. I'd be
interested to know.'

Peter Ferry, a curious reader

'Sirs, Berry Tonge, like many folk outside the System, have to
have money to live. As one connected with his practical life I
can say that he was basically worried about money. It is ironical
that only a short while ago he presented to our Speakers'
Agency a new title *A Bowl of Rice Will Do*.
　'The Book Industry for instance wanted him to give one of
his well-loved talks – *Read Your Way to Riches*. They said they
couldn't afford a fee. He refused to speak and got me to write to
them saying that he "would prostitute himself no longer."
　'Yes, Berry Tonge was an angry man. But he was a talented
man. Hid first book, written as a young man – *Speak Out!* –
went to seven editions and is still a valuable text for those
wanting a vocation as a public speaker. He was a "broadcaster"
and one of the first so to describe himself.
　'He was an authority on Fruitful Co-partnership in Industry,
but met with puzzled apathy from both unions and
management.
　'I look sadly into his file and see that his spare-time interests
are listed as "conversation, bread baking, and care of the garden
and all that in it dwells."

'I see he gave us one title on human relations which was called *A Shoulder is to Cry On as well as for the Wheel*. There will be a great many people who will wish they'd known to offer him a shoulder.'

June T. Dempster (Mrs), June T. Dempster Speakers' Agency Ltd

'Sirs, A short letter to convey my disgust at the way you wrote about Berry Tonge. If Berry could have read that obituary he would no doubt have felt like dying again.

As usual Blase wrote about himself. Count how many times the pronoun I is used – 23.'

Teresa Grey

LETTERS, MARCH 20

'Sirs, What an enormous lot of superstitious and sentimental plain old silly rubbish your letters have been about Berry Tonge. Yet you have a note threatening to cut long, boring letters and to axe short, boring letters. Why was this policy suspended?

'Perhaps all this is inevitable in this pseudo-scientific age, with apothegms of the past becoming superstitious folk sayings of the present. This new age of illiteracy has turned us back into yelping savages when we cannot longer disregard the phrase "Speak No Ill of the Dead."

'I myself am a Public Speaker (why did Berry Tonge drop this age-honourable title for the fashionable, silly title Free Teacher?). As a Public Speaker I do not feel Berry Tonge was above criticism, in enunciation especially. Whether he was a good speaker is a matter for discussion at any time. The Great

Leveller is not also the Great Censor. As a rationalist also I will
not be intimidated by death.'

Peter Smith

'Sirs, I think the obituary for Berry Tonge was most beautiful.
But maybe there is something the matter with me? Surely those
who complain could feel the pain. Facetious – no! Read again
the last line . . . it said it all.'

R. Harley

LETTERS, MARCH 27

'Sirs, Now we've had it all. Sentimental signatories, the
slightly acid obituary – readers for and against.
    'I knew Berry Tonge rather better in a way than others.
Recognising what the poor bugger was up against, I did my
best to flog his last book *Some Words for the Young*. It must have
sold in all about 50 copies. It was not a good book and I told
him (the reviewer for your newspaper was the only one who
praised it).
    'Berry Terminated because like so many of us who do the
same, he could not use his failure in one direction as an
experience to build success in another sphere. That was it. It
amazes me that the others who knew Berry don't see this.
    'There are still 230 copies of his book in my shop. Should
any of those who wrote to say how much they cared for Berry,
like to buy them I'll give the money towards a scholarship in
his name (less the cost of the books to me initially).'

Signed, Wholemeal Books Ltd

APRIL 4

from the vineyard
It seems many of my readers and colleagues have been deeply
offended by my 'passing' remarks on the death of Berry Tonge.
I am not sure whether it was because I spoke the truth or
because I tried to be humorous about death. Why not?

To those who say I was facetious I can then but plead guilty
. . . but only in order not to weep. And as for speaking the truth
– guilty, friends, guilty. But I was not writing your customary
accolade or epitaph for Berry Tonge. That is not our way here.

I do not know if any of you have read you own writings in
the still of the night, as I have, and had that cold feeling that
you were really never going to make it. I have. All I suggested is
that is what Berry Tonge did.

Young Morris has a nice story about Tonge's 'Flexible Love',
which Berry suggests they both experience in the lavatory here
at the office. Young Morris says he wasn't feeling that flexible.

And I will say they can write whatever obituaries they like,
but they know bugger all about the proper way to say goodbye
to a fellow toiler in the vineyard writing week in week out
about life's rich pageant, weaving threads in the tapestry of life,
a tapestry one is never destined to see.

What a heartbreak old vineyard, pageant, and tapestry you
are.

Blase

LETTERS, APRIL 11

'Sir, Thank you Francois Blase for replying to those who
whinge about your Berry Tonge obit. Better the truth than the
bullshit. Especially at death.

'Many hours of pleasure your writings have given me too.

I'll never forget the insect dropping his bright green turd down the stem of your pipe. The book reviews terribly good also.

'And you other bastards stop writing whingeing letters and recognise the truth when you see it. Especially about death. And Berry Tonge especially.'

Heinz Laverte

'Sirs, Maybe T. S. Eliot, the poet, can be allowed the last and lingering words on the death of Berry Tonge:

Berry was much posssessed by death
And saw the skull beneath the skin . . .
He knew the anguish of the sorrow
The ague of the skeleton;
No contact possible with the flesh
Allayed the bone.

'As one who knew Berry Tonge, I think that his poem answers the "all he needed was a shoulder to cry on" letter writers.'

Percy Routage

'Sirs, So much for the self-claimed honesty of this Francois Blase. In the obituary (March 6) he says that he never reads his own writing and then on April 9 in his abject apology, he says he does read his own writing.

'I think he now stands exposed.'

One of the Seven

'Sirs, Your paper has caused me much anguish over the last weeks, with its bickering over the death of Berry Tonge. I was in his Encounter Group which still has three meetings to go. As

Leader of the Group, Berry Tonge kept me going with his
words and exuded love. He was always able to say something
apt.

'Now you tell me that he has taken his own life. Can this be
some sort of joke? I must say I scarcely understand the humour
of your paper.

'What of me and the Encounter Group? Can your poets and
clever readers tell me where this leaves me vis-a-vis Berry
Tonge and his Philosophy? This is Not a Joke.'

(Name withheld by request)

Discussion of this subject is now concluded. Ed.

THE LAST OF THE PUBLIC IDLERS
....
AND LAUNDROMAT COMMUNALISTS
....

Notes:
For the old *Thor* and then for the *Bulletin* I wrote a column
called 'Around the Laundromats' – a commentary on inner-city
living. But Westinghouse objected to the use of the word
Laundromat in the column, it being a trade name and not a
common noun. The column in that format came to an end.
I include one column for sake of the record and because it was a
column I loved to write.

Ward and I were sitting in the laundromat in our sweaters,
swimming shorts, shoes without socks, along with the rest of
the Balmainians, who had all their washable clothes in the
machines.

Bill Beard the Balmain Poet says that laundromats should be
nudist so that one could wash everything. Laundry is a meta-
phorical shedding of skins.

It had been raining that week and consequently the laundromat was like a congested nose with non-laundromat mothers
using the driers for their nappies.

One of the laundromat TV-club was there – people who spread their laundry over a few nights to watch the TV because they don't own a set.

'You know,' I said to Ward, 'people are more and more dropping off their laundry to be done rather than doing it themselves. It's killing off the village communal laundry spirit. The spirit of the laundromat.'

'Who gives a stuff?' said Ward, who has no sentimentality. 'People who haven't time to sit around their village laundromat yarning must lead very urgent lives,' I said. 'They also miss out on the ritual of rejuvenation. It is the decline of public idleness.'

'Who gives a stuff?' said Ward.

'But in old photographs of the city you see people lounging on park benches, sitting in the gutter, leaning against verandah poles.'

'Unemployment,' said Ward, 'you'll see the photographs again.'

'I suppose this year at Orientation Week at the University they won't have the Gay Kissing stall,' I said. 'Remember the 50 cents To-Kiss-a-Gay stall?'

I felt nostalgic. 'Everything's changing.'

Ward snorted.

'The year before, the Gay Liberationists ran the fairy-floss machine at the University of New South Wales: "Get your fairy floss from a real fairy." I guess that won't be there either.'

I pointed out to Ward that a guy was washing his 'White Power' National Action T-shirt while at the same time in the adjoining machine a Land Rights T-shirt was going through. We get a lot of messages in the Balmain laundromat.

'The laundromat is neutral,' I remarked thoughtfully.

'Everyone gets dirty,' Ward said.

'Elemental bonding,' I said, 'the dirty laundry attests to our common mong.'

'Overload,' Ward said, nodding at our machine.

The drum out-of-balance light came on and there was an

embarrassing noisy, thumping, as the Norge came to a concentric stop. I'd tried to fit our laundry in two machines. I was embarrassed by this display of laundromat incompetence but no one looked. People never look at each other's laundry.

The TV, the old magazines, are all what Irving Goffman called 'involvement shields'.

Although the laundromat is a 'loose situation' in that you can wear whatever you want, it is also the performance of a personal act in a public place.

It is, consequently, not a place for eye contact or face engagement; you should not, as an act of propriety, look at other people's dirty laundry.

This would be a 'situational impropriety'.

This was why Ward and I felt unable to tell the young man not to put bleach in with his blankets. To do this would be to let on that we were watching him – were laundry pervs.

If you take newspapers into a laundromat they are taken when you go over to your machine because people treat all reading matter as communal in the laundromat.

I spread the laundry over three machines this time.

We sat there grooving on a three-machine wash and all its rhythm.

'You know Ward, we should always have a three-machine wash – it is a better show. All that machinery pounding away for us.'

The cycles of the three machines were in unison like the click-clack of three tap dancers.

'What do you use with coloureds?' Ward queried.

The question surprised me, we were both laundromat experts. 'Warm wash, cold rinse, no bleach,' I said.

'No,' he said, with a black smile, 'cattle prods.'

I groaned, 'You can be gaoled for that now – now that virtue is to be imposed by pious tribunals.'

I told Ward that the Norge washing machines were made in Alabama, by black labour.

'So what?'

'Well, Professor Knight pointed out that as a joke the machine is called "Norge", which is an anagram of negro.'

Ward drew my attention to a couple both wearing Nuclear Disarmament badges. 'You notice,' Ward said, 'she operates the washing machines, loads it and puts in the soap, while he holds the baby, but when she returns, he hands her the baby and goes on reading his magazine. He doesn't get off his arse.'

'But he's only here to hold the baby while she puts the washing in the machine – and to carry the laundry home – that's his job,' I said.

The soap dispenser had begun to run uncontrollably. There was no attendant around. We all just looked at it. All of us had machines going and couldn't benefit from the free soap. It reminded me of the fable about the salt-making machine which would not stop and which the owner threw into the sea, thus giving us salt water.

Ward and I talked about the bicentenary — Ward believed it to be an ideal time for us to abandon the flag and the anthem.

'As a contribution to internationalism?' I said, 'Cute'.

'No', said Ward with disgust, 'as a contribution to tribalism. There is no bloody nation. We have to acknowledge the identities of smaller groups.'

We went over to the coffee vendo-mat for a break.
We put our wash into the driers checking that we hadn't left any socks behind.

People came and went, leaving their laundry to be done. The attendant had now fixed the broken soap-dispenser.

For a time, Ward and I had hoped that the laundromat was the beginning of the New Communalism – a movement away from a million little people doing a million little washes in a million little machines. We hoped for a re-birth of village life around the laundromat.

Whitlam had wanted it. Maybe if he'd stayed on ...

We went to get our clothes from the dryer – as usual the jeans and towels were still a trifle damp.

Ward searched the driers for loose change which might have fallen from our clothing pockets. Or anyone's clothing.

Silently we stuffed the cleaned clothes into the blue laundry bags and walked home – the last of the laundromat communalists and public idlers.

FRANCOIS AND THE FISHBONE INCIDENT

This is a cautionary tale and a test. The cautionary tale is for bon vivants and the test is for cadet journalists.

In the role of Francois Blase, bon vivant and celebrated author, I was celebrating the publication of my latest book and had gathered around me my closest friends, Rosemary Creswell, my agent, and Murray Sime, my taxation lawyer – a far-sighted combination, even if it does indicate a certain limitation in human relationships on my part. We were in a merry mood, the champagne flowing, they doing private calculations in their heads (they together own 20 per cent of my life), and I on my feet making a fine speech, when a snapper bone in my throat stopped me in mid-flourish.

At first this seemed very funny for my luncheon guests, who fell into indulgent, but hearty laughter.

They laughed while I, caught mid-word, champagne glass in hand, began to stagger backwards, choking.

After their laughter died down they began exuberant back-slapping and folk remedies such as swallowing bread (I was later to learn that bread sometimes breaks the fishbone off leaving a piece of bone embedded in the throat). I went on choking.

At last, their meal ticket dying before their eyes, my friends became serious. The restaurant kindly put the snapper back in the oven and, champagne glass in hand, tears in my eyes, Murray walked me across the road to Balmain Hospital. I remembered that the singer Mama Cass choked to death on a ham sandwich.

He signed me in and went back to finish his lunch with Rosemary, my only consolation being that one of them had to pay.

The young doctor in Casualty well understood my problem, but said there was little that could be done 'manually'. However, he said cheerfully that he'd read my books and they were terrific.

Finding it difficult to talk I simply kissed his hands appreciatively.

As he wheeled me to the Ear, Nose and Throat specialist he talked about the books, but the more he talked the more it became obvious that the book he was talking about was not my book *The Americans, Baby*, but Craig McGregor's *Up Against the Wall, America*.

Being unable to correct him, I could only nod glumly, smile weakly, gesture impotently.

I thought: I am going to die a bizarre newsworthy death like Mama Cass, and Craig McGregor is going to get all the publicity.

The young doctor got onto jazz – evidently McGregor wrote about jazz – and then left, giving me a thumbs-up gesture and saying, 'You can give me a 12-string Gibson anytime you like.'

A 12-string Gibson???!!! a 12-string Gibson . . . ???

I've drunk a Gibson, but I've never played a Gibson.

While I waited for the specialist I noticed that my name had been mis-spelled, but at least it wasn't down as McGregor. My name is so often mis-spelled I may as well change it to Francois Blase.

The specialist squirted anaesthetic into my throat, which made me feel even sicker, and then tried manually to locate the bone, but failed because my throat kept expelling him and his instruments.

He accused me of being tense.

He concluded that he would have to put me under a full anaesthetic and operate. As punishment for being tense.

He wrote my name down, mis-spelled it, asked me my date of birth and wrongly calculated that I was 32, which at first was alright by me, but then worried me because I feared that the dose of anaesthetic was calculated by age and that I would die from an overdose, or worse, I would receive an 'under dose' which would immobilise me, but not kill the pain. I would lie there, unable to move or speak, while they operated and I felt it all.

I was wheeled by a nurse to the Admissions Office where I was asked questions that I could not answer – not only was I having trouble vocally, but the questions, while technically quite simple, could not adequately snare the mess of my life.

She asked me for my next-of-kin and I hesitated because my parents were holidaying in the Pacific Islands so it would be useless to name them; but even if they were home they wouldn't know who Craig McGregor was when the police called with the bad news.

'What about wife?' she asked. Well, I was married very young and I have never bothered to get divorced, although we had lived apart for years and she is living in London. I couldn't explain this to her, but to say 'yes' to 'married' meant that I had to give my wife's address, which I didn't have. I shook my head in reply to the question which was technically a lie, but more the truth – if you know what I mean.

I began to give my father as next-of-kin, but she asked me for his address and telephone number, which I did not know, but had written in my address book, which I did not have. She looked at me severely and put down 'care of the police'.

She asked me what rent I paid, and I didn't know because I pay a year in advance. I wanted to say, 'Look I'm dying here, can we do the questions when I'm being discharged?'

She asked me which medical fund I belonged to and I couldn't remember.

She asked me my weekly wage and I couldn't answer because I don't have a weekly wage, but I was now so desperate to have an answer to something that I invented a figure. She seemed to disbelieve me anyhow.

She was by now suspicious of my identity and asked me in a pointed tone who Francois Blase was. Murray as some sort of joke had written Francois Blase in brackets or vice versa on the form *he* filled in.

I am drowning in saliva. I am slipping into shock, my heart is racing, my skin is cold.

I made an agonised face at her and spelled out silently 'J-O-K-E'. She sniffed.

She decided to let me into the hospital, however, despite my unsatisfactory mark in the Admission Exam.

While being wheeled back to the ward I pondered the technical question of 'who am I' and so forth – every piece of information in the hands of the hospital was now either wrong, dysfunctional, or to my disadvantage. Some was technically correct, but misleading; some technically wrong, but true.

I was next dressed in surgical gown, leggings and a surgical nappy and an identity bracelet placed on my wrist.

I was very glad to see the bracelet. It said my name was 'Moorehouse', my age was 36, and the address on the bracelet was not my home address, but the address of the Volunteer Restaurant where I had been having lunch.

I was rather desperate to clear up the age question because I had convinced myself that this was crucial in determining drug dosage.

But if I did die, my next-of-kin would not be at home, my body would be delivered to a restaurant, and Craig McGregor would get all the publicity.

The nursing aides who dressed me in the operating gown asked me if I was married. Were the trying to trick me into giving the 'correct' answer – were they in conspiracy with the admissions clerk?

If I wasn't married, why not?

Was this aimed to determine if I was homosexual – and what different sorts of treatment did homosexuals get? Better treatment or worse? What about AIDS? Would I be put in an airtight, isolated room and handled only be remote-control, bionic arms?

If I were 36, which I wasn't, and unmarried, was I therefore suspected of homosexuality and treated thus? I told them I was married. Would they like me to contact my wife? No. Why not?

I saw then, quite clearly, poetically, that the whole world, every one of us, is adrift in a sea of misinformation and misunderstanding.

A Resident came to my bed and asked me more questions. He asked me, for instance, when I was last in hospital, which I mis-answered unintentionally because I had forgotten about an incident in the country thirteen years ago. I told him my correct age and he wrote it down, but what about all the other forms – would it be corrected on those as well? He looked at me oddly and wrote something on his sheet which I feared was against me.

I lied to him about the food I'd eaten that day because I couldn't bring myself to tell him I'd had a Big Mac and a beer for breakfast. Francois Blase is happy to tell the doctor about the Moet champagne and the kidneys in wine for lunch, but he can't bring himself to tell about the Big Mac. But it wasn't only snobbery. It would again be dangerously misleading to tell him about the beer and the Big Mac. I had never before in my life had a beer and a Big Mac for breakfast. He would assume that I had a bad diet and was an alcoholic. A train of medical assumptions would follow and I would be put on the wrong drip and given the wrong dosages of all sorts of things.

How I came to have a Big Mac and beer for breakfast would take a long time to explain. This was a case where the correct information could be dangerously misleading, so I lied about breakfast.

All the way to the operating theatre I believed that I had been mistaken for someone else – some other 'Moorhouse' or 'Moorshouse' or 'Moorehouse' who had gangrene and was to have his leg amputated. Or a certain 'Francois' who had AIDS.

I indicated over and over again to the wardsman, the nurse, the anaesthetist and the specialist that I had a bone in my throat and please not my leg, or whatever they amputate in cases of AIDS. I used emphatic gesticulation and mime – mimed a swimming fish with my hand, mimed eating with a knife and fork, I gave a great re-enactment of me giving a speech, pain in the throat, choking.

The operation found no fishbone, but they said they could see where it had been.

A few days later, when I visited the specialist for a check-up, he found that he had no card for me.

That did not surprise me.

But then he said, 'Oh this must be you,' looking at a card, 'it's the right complaint, but the wrong name.' How would he know that? I didn't ask if the name he had was Francois McGregor. I didn't care.

He told me that bon vivants should not order fish when they are in an excited or celebratory mood.

Now for the test for cadet journalists. How would you get the correct name, age, and address of the patient, given that the doctor in Casualty would have been genuinely helpful and told you I was Craig McGregor.

It would have been no good asking the patient when he had a

fishbone stuck in his throat, was in philosophical confusion
about his identity, saw himself as Francois Blase, bon vivant,
and thought he was dying like Mama Cass.

BLASE AT LAKE EYRE

Well Chief, there was movement at the restaurant when the word passed around that Francois Blase, the Balmain Bushman, was going to Lake Eyre.

You bet.

I'd been talking up my bush skills, I suppose, around Kinselas, EJs, Berowra Waters, Fannys, Florentinos and I suppose someone took me seriously at last and they've invited me to join an expedition to the Lake. Susie from EJs is demanding that I settle the slate before I go – not very French of her – I wrote a draft of one of my pieces on a tablecloth in way of payment, but she didn't think much of that.

Enclosed is the EJs account which I'd be pleased if you could settle against future earnings together with letter to be opened in case of death.

You may have heard that the Lake has filled with water for the second time in 200 years and with this fashionable concern with the environment I thought you might like to style me as 'ecology writer' or something like that – it would help me to ingratiate myself with the young chicks (memo sub-editor: delete that from published copy, thanks).

About insurance: double it. Dr C.T. Madigan tells me that
the Lake is 'under the evil influence of Kuddimurkra, a djinn-
like spirit which may appear in the form of a giant snake with
the head of the Kangaroo, likely to do much harm to the
unwary traveller.'

Of course, I intend packing a bottle or two of white-man's
magic – 'a gin-like spirit' – like it?

The expedition is made up of city folk, ABC producers and
the like, and they are not at ease in the wilds. The planning session was carefully left 'unstructured' I gather, and was, as you'd
expect, very aware to the New Sensitivities. In a laid back sort
of way.

'Let's watch the sex roles emerge out there in the desert,' said
Janet, an ABC producer, which is an example of what I mean.
However there were some Old Sensitivities discussed as well,
like toilet arrangements and nakedness.

Bill, a sociologist, was for everyone being naked and eating
raw vegetables.

I'm a purist in my own way, Chief, as you know, but about
the wilderness I like to do it the high-tech route. Plenty of
Swiss Army gear and Gore-tex and star-gazer tents. You can
hold the Velcro though – don't care for that noise of raw pain
in the morning.

I said that as for toilet, nakedness and diet I was not prepared
to participate in any consciousness-raising or reconditioning
exercise in personal liberation. I said, perhaps bad-humouredly,
that I had trouble enough with what liberation I already had.
And that my consciousness was uncomfortably raised. I have to
report a few horse laughs at this.

I also muttered, but was not heard, perhaps all for the better,
that too many people had 'high self-esteem' and that most
people were quite correct in having low self-esteem.

As something of a hunter, I broached the subject of bringing
along my old Winchester over and under 12 gauge. I found
that this was another sensitivity. I painted them a picture of

living off the land, fishing and shooting, cooking wild ducks in gin and juniper sauce or with Colonel Hawker's sauce. Or some snowshoe rabbit and applejack, and I do a mean snipe straight off the skillet.

But the planning session demurred. They have inhibitions about me toting a Winchester and definitely vetoed my wearing of the customary side arm.

They were attracted to the Living-Off-the-Land Ethic, but unable to reconcile it with their Conservationist Ethic. I stated bluntly that I was untroubled by either ethic and told them a little about the doctrine of *ferae naturae,* that there is no property in wild birds and animals, that they belonged to all for food and for their beauty.

' "Every moving thing that liveth shall be meat for you," ' I quoted to them, but the Bible doesn't seem to impress any more.

There were rumblings too about my ability to feed the party.

Still, if they wouldn't allow me to shoot I said that I would snare animals and birds and showed them my piano wire – a few lethal jerks and a couple of lethal knots. Some of the party found this disquieting, I could tell, and would have preferred it if I were not going to the Lake with them. Bloody left-liberals. Hemingway where are you.

They all talked of 'travelling light', which is all very well I suppose, but I believe in camp-de-luxe wherever possible – take as much as you can carry.

For instance, Chief, I always carry my brass Alpinist's lantern for the tent, not only for the warm, mellow glow, but because it has a brass ring for warming the eight-ounce brandy snifter. Get what I mean?

And I carry a pillow. So did the great bushman George W. Sears.

Well, they were all for travelling light, so I let them.

No one raised, of course, the question of leadership. In these days of anti-elitism the question of leadership was undiscussable and I went home from the planning sessions quietly disappointed that they hadn't appointed, someone, myself maybe, as Expedition Captain, say – nothing grand.

One of the party said that 'We are all generals these days,' which really means 'We would all wish to be generals', but how many of us really are when it's down to the line?

Well, we flew the 1600 kilometres inland in a chartered twelve-seater Piaggio to the-dead-heart-which-now-lived, the mythical inland sea, the place which the explorers died searching for, this mysterious inland, the communal unconscious, the fabled outback. During the flight I made a speech from the aisle of the plane.

I said that I saw the expedition as a 're-birth trauma' where we were to take our bodies almost to the point of death and then back to life. The others disagreed and talked about alleged interest in wild-life and geography and ecology.

'Well, I intend to immerse myself in the life water of the continent and be baptised as a true Australian,' I said, feeling at the time deeply moved. I told them that all the Australian explorers had been superficially scientific, but more driven by curiosity, romance, and the desire to take oneself to the edge of death.

The others said they had no intention to take themselves 'to the edge of death'. I retired then to the back of the aircraft with a bottle of white-man's magic.

Almost to a person the dress was denim. I alone wore moleskins and I alone had on my belt pouches for my barometer, compass, and watch – as well as my Puma Hunter's Companion sheath knife. I wore my empty forty-five holster as a protest, which would, in a time of crisis, when a forty-five might be a comfort, make a point to all the bleeding-heart liberals.

There were one hell of a lot of Adidas shoes.

Donald Stuart, the author-bushman, now in his sixties, wore an Arabic robe and went barefoot. He'd been toughened up in

Pilbara while the rest of us had been softened up in Kinselas. I sure envied him his style, Chief.

There were more Swiss Army knives than you could poke through the holes of a Swiss cheese. I was still waiting for my custom-made knife from Victurinox.

All of them feared the dreaded bush rats described by early explorers to the region. I must also say, that I did not fancy making camp in a rat plague. I had in mind the digging of a moat, but I would have liked the ole-six-shooter. Don't like rats.

After landing, we were driven by truck forty kilometres to the Lake and left there with a pile of firewood – the Lake country is sand-dune with knee-high scrub – OK for a blaze but not for a proper cooking fire.

I was pleased and disconcerted as a hunter to see that the rabbits at the Lake were fat and orange, which seemed to contradict the laws of survival about merging with the environment. The others could see them *too*.

I got out the piano wire, but again met the worried frowns of the other members of the party.

My plan for a ceremony of immersion in the Holy Lake (Chief, I am not without some spirituality you know) was impeded, if not desecrated by sight and stench of thousands of rotting fish – bony bream – strewn along the Lake's beach line for hundreds of kilometres into the distance. Aw hell, instead of a testament to the recuperative power and abundance of nature, instead of purity, I was faced with death – worse, wasteful slaughter of life, the rotting of the flesh, the self-wounding capacity of nature. What was I to do, Chief? This wasn't the first time that Australian wilderness had played its little joke on me. All that the Australian wilderness has ever said to me is 'Life's tough, mate.'

I want a more affirmative statement from nature.

I suppose I was let down by it – the joke of the stinking fish – and kicked the sand, but I mixed myself a bloody mary (much to the contemptuous amusement of the bleeding liberals who were all now nature freaks) and calmed down.

(The bloody marys were pre-mixed by the Company of Two, Fresno, California – sub-editor, please leave in brand name, OK? Wink, wink).

The Lake was also jumping with fish, if that was nature's attempt at an ambiguous statement. We had a water scientist with us, Marike, and she said that the lake was increasing its salinity as the fresh water which has filled it absorbs salt from the soil and at the same time evaporates. By the way, where do the fish all come from so quickly? Who tells the fish and the birds that it's all happening at Lake Eyre? That's a mystery, Chief. There may be an explanation, but I'm leaving that a holy mystery.

Marike did some tests. We do not stand in awe. We do some tests. Anyway, who could stand in awe of ten billion stinking fish which smell like Bombay Duck. Or just Bombay. She said that the Lake now had the same salinity as the sea. The jumping fish we were seeing were probably not frolicking or saluting the Miracle of the Lake, they were trying to *get out*.

I recorded in my field log that the water was soft, that is, contained no calcium salts which prevent soap lathering, that it had a high buoyancy from the salt, no current, of course, and a tepid temperature. Very benign, said Robert, a stock and station man. Since when do stock and station men get to say poetry?

But when whipped by wind, we were to see, the Lake can raise waves as high as thirty centimetres. Is that enough reporting, Chief? Can I get on with more important existential questions now?

The thing which excited me as a hunter and gatherer was the heavy animal, bird, and insect traffic in the sand. I am something of an expert scat reader and it was the equivalent of *War and Peace* for a scat reader. I was relieved to find no Broad-toothed Rat *(Mastacomys fuscus)* or the dreaded Black Rat *(Rattus rattus)*. The Lake teemed with black swans, herons, pelicans and ducks but they all stayed out of snaring range. Word travels fast.

I was putting together my demountable bush deck-chair which packs away into a pack the size of a paperback book, when I heard the cry, 'Blase! Quickly, a snake!'

I said to myself, but not in the hearing of the others, 'Kuddimurkra'. I had been expecting the djinn-like spirit of the Lake. The Aboriginal Spirit of anti-tourism.

I went to where they were standing transfixed by a very long and very big fawn-coloured snake with ominous markings on its head. I moved them back away from the snake with my outspread arms. I then crouched and examined it. I picked it for a collared brown snake. They move very quickly. Easily aroused. When antagonised will strike repeatedly. Uses a very powerful neurotoxin. You could say that the collared brown snake 'goes for it.'

'For Godsake do something, Blase!' they cried.

At last they needed a Leader. Ha ha. At last they realised the value of a man who can handle himself in the wilds. They would wish they had let me bring my forty-five.

'We're eighty kilometres from medical attention, Blase.'
I walked down to the edge of the Lake to give myself time to think through the problem. The others stood in a frightened, huddled group. The snake watched me, having rightly sensed where its match lay, from whence combat would come.

It was not just a snake. This would be a ritual slaying. I squatted down and bathed my arms in the Lake up to the armpits.

Some of the party had gone to their tents for their cameras.

When I go into action, I thought, I had better be damned good. This was going to get around Kinselas.

I stripped to the waist and selected an Estwing Number 2 half axe manufactured in Illinois, and adopted the mien of a warrior.

I first built a blind from a thicket of desert scrub and then,

going some distance out from the snake, began to stalk my way
in behind this mobile blind. Patience and stealth, Chief.

After a while the party drifted away with their cameras to
play chess and to read Burke and Wills and so on.

After eight hours of stalking I approached the place where
the snake was last seen and found it to be gone. It had
apparently lost patience and gone to its hole. What sort of
collared brown snake takes off like that? I threw away my blind
in a fury and shouted at it down its hole, 'Come out and fight!'

I gathered the party around me and told them that it was a
'tactical victory'. Bloodshed had been avoided and the snake
was gone. I explained that the party should make as much noise
and movement as possible to keep it guessing.

I said that I'd established a concord with the snake, 'The
snake sensed my capacity to kill it, but at the same time my
reservations about the need to kill it. The snake, however, was
not in doubt as to my *will* to kill. Having computed this the
snake decided to sit it out. I got through to the snake – there
was dialogue occurring out there.'

I felt like Howard Hunter of the Desert Hill Street Precinct.

The party divided into those who sat around the camp fire
and those who sat around porta-gas lamps.

It's all about tight and loose communication. The lamp is a
defined and intense focus while the camp fire is diffuse. You
see, the fire allows you to sit in the half light or dark and have a
low presence both to others and yourself. The fire allows you to
receive signals from the outer darkness because the fire light
and the darkness imperceptibly meet and merge; it allows the
noises of the outer darkness to come to you. The fire makes a
shapeless, but contained play of light which gets up things
from the unconscious and it's a sort of mental plasticine too
which you can turn into a TV screen of the psyche.

The bright light, however, defines clearly the circle of
attention, everyone is defined, and it excludes the stimuli of the
night, creates hard-edged conversation.

That night it rained. Sometimes it doesn't rain for ten years at Lake Eyre, but in the night a pattering soft rain began.

I roused everyone from their tents telling them that they had to 'bare themselves' to the event. They were a complaining bunch and immediately began to fear that it would mean flooding and the trucks might not be able to make it in to collect us. They had a point. I took an inventory of our supplies and suggested that as from the next morning we all go onto half rations.

By morning however, the rains had gone. The desert was as dry as a desert should be.

I had spent the night sponging water from the sides of the tents and squeezing it into an emergency tank. My presence around the tents during the night brought me some abuse, but as Leader I had a duty to maximise our chances of survival.

They would've been glad of that water if we'd been stuck there for ten months.

But the trucks came and I lowered the flag and struck camp. Before leaving I went to the snake hole and said farewell. Back at EJs I bemoaned to Susie that we hadn't had a proper rebirth trauma and that there had been insufficient hardship experienced. She said that not everyone courted danger like I did. I suppose she's right.

She suggested that maybe now that I was back in the city I should give up wearing the boots, leggings, moleskins, barometer pouch, compass pouch, windchill factor gauge pouch, and stop eating in public with a bone-handled sheath knife. I told her I was having trouble re-adjusting to city ways.

AUTHOR'S NOTE AND ACKNOWLEDGEMENTS
....

None of these pieces have appeared together in book form and all have been revised for this book.

Most of the Francois Blase pieces appeared in the *Bulletin* or *Business Review Weekly*. The Oral History of Childhood pieces, 'Mechanical Aptitude' and 'Jealousy Tests', appeared in the *National Times,* and 'Pledges and Vows' in *The Hard Word*. 'The Drover's Wife' was first broadcast over the ABC as a mock item in a program called 'The Anzacs and All That' and later published in the *Bulletin*.

'An Incident from the Wake for Jack Kerouac' appeared in *Coast-to-Coast*, 'The Subject of Death is now Concluded' first appeared in *Quadrant*. 'Around the Laundromats' was a column which appeared in *Thor* and then in the *Bulletin*. 'Convalescence' appeared in *Stand* as 'Dirty Girl'. Some of the pieces have not been previously published.

Permission to reproduce the items in the article 'The Drover's Wife' is gratefully acknowledged: the *Bulletin*, the *National Times,* and the individual sources named.

MEMORIES OF THE ASSASSINATION ATTEMPT AND OTHER STORIES

Gerard Windsor

A man spars with his wife over his dead mother-in-law's unopened wedding presents; a deserted woman is visited by the father of her child; an old priest relives a tragedy in which his own youthful idealism was instrumental; an urbane gynaecologist discovers there are some parts of his women that retaliate . . .

The reach and range of Gerard Windsor's imagination has already been critically acclaimed: 'fabulist, moralist and humorist all at once'. His stories reflect experiences that span the sensual to the spiritual, the mundane to the macabre, yet beneath all their irony lurk subtle compassion and moral concern. This fine new collection can only assure his reputation as one of Australia's most deft and engaging fiction writers.

IKONS

A collection of stories

George Papaellinas

Even after thirty years, the Mavromatis family cannot understand their life in Australia. Until Peter Mavromatis's first exhibition as an 'ethnic' photographer clarifies everything.

In this collection of stories we follow the family fortunes. Old Yiayia has already lived her life in the old country. Christos and Eli wage a private war as confused as the motives which brought them from Cyprus. For Peter, their Australian-born son and proud hope for the future, life is a contest of shallow cultural identities and allegiances.

Ikons is a vivid and contentious protrayal of a family united only by society's view of them as outsiders.

Also published by Penguin

THE STATE OF THE ART

Introduced and edited by Frank Moorhouse

A frenetic, talented guitarist, barely hanging on to a
fragmented life; a canny Jewish uncle, frustrated without
a family to organise; lovers seeking pleasure. Whatever the
cost; an old woman, trundled from the home of one son to
another, an intrusion, unloved . . .

These are among the characters, some innocent, some
eccentric, some disillusioned, who are portrayed in this
striking, innovative collection of short stories. Their
diversity of style and content reflects the robust hedonism
of contemporary Australian society.

TRANSGRESSIONS

Australian Writing Now

Edited by Don Anderson

Woman marries dog
Farnarkeling – state of play
Top odds at country race meeting
Conflict between black tribal law and white 'justice'

Not the news, but the newest and best in recent short prose
– the state of Australian writing today by both established
masters of the craft and newer writers.

Don Anderson has chosen work by authors like Carmel
Bird, Barbara Brooks, Beverley Farmer, Helen Garner,
Susan Hampton, Elizabeth Jolley, Richard Lunn, David
Malouf and Frank Moorhouse for this excitingly various
collection.

Here you will find the traditional at its most eminent and
original, the leading edge at its most cutting and innovative.